# Sunrise

# by

# Kathi Daley

I want to thank the very talented Jessica Fischer for the cover art.

I so appreciate Bruce Curran, who is always ready and willing to answer my cyber questions.

And, of course, thanks to the readers and bloggers in my life, who make doing what I do possible.

Thank you to Randy Ladenheim-Gil for the editing.

Special thanks to Jeannie Daniel, Janel Flynn, Wanda Philmon Downs, and Pam Curran for submitting recipes.

And finally I want to thank my sister Christy for always lending an ear and my husband Ken for allowing me time to write by taking care of everything else.

# Books by Kathi Daley

Come for the murder, stay for the romance.

## Zoe Donovan Cozy Mystery:

Halloween Hijinks
The Trouble With Turkeys
Christmas Crazy
Cupid's Curse
Big Bunny Bump-off
Beach Blanket Barbie
Maui Madness
Derby Divas
Haunted Hamlet
Turkeys, Tuxes, and Tabbies
Christmas Cozy
Alaskan Alliance
Matrimony Meltdown
Soul Surrender
Heavenly Honeymoon
Hopscotch Homicide
Ghostly Graveyard
Santa Sleuth
Shamrock Shenanigans
Kitten Kaboodle

# Tj Jensen Paradise Lake Series

Pumpkins in Paradise – Sept. 2016
Snowmen in Paradise – Sept 2016
Bikinis in Paradise – Sept 2016
Christmas in Paradise – Sept 2016
Puppies in Paradise – Sept 2016
Halloween in Paradise – Sept 2016
Treasure in Paradise – April 2017

# Whales and Tails Cozy Mystery:

Romeow and Juliet
The Mad Catter
Grimm's Furry Tail
Much Ado About Felines
Legend of Tabby Hollow
Cat of Christmas Past
A Tale of Two Tabbies
The Great Catsby – *July 2016*

# Seacliff High Mystery:

The Secret
The Curse
The Relic
The Conspiracy
The Grudge

# Sand and Sea Hawaiian Mystery:

Murder at Dolphin Bay
Murder at Sunrise

# Road to Christmas Romance:

Road to Christmas Past

# Chapter 1

## Monday, June 20

There was a hush among the group of twenty seniors gathered in the predawn hours to greet the summer solstice. I had been invited to join the celebration by my next-door neighbor, Elva Talbot, who was dependent on me and others in her life for transportation. Each of the twenty-one people in attendance were equipped with a conch shell that would be sounded in harmony as the first rays of the summer sun appeared over the horizon. In Hawaii the sounding of the conch is a tradition used to announce important moments such as a sunrise or sunset, a ceremony such as a wedding, or the arrival of royalty or an important person. The beautiful and haunting sound could carry up to two miles and at times the shells were blown to the north, south, east, and west, signifying all the powers.

"He came," Elva whispered in my ear as a man who looked to be in his late sixties joined the group. I knew he was new to the island and had caught the eye of my neighbor when he joined the group of seniors who recreated together on a regular basis.

"The man you told me you wanted to invite to the dance at the senior center?"

Elva nodded.

"So introduce us," I whispered back.

Elva blushed and looked as if she was going to refuse. I grabbed her hand and walked toward the tall man with the thin face, beaklike nose, and white hair. Dressed in a dark suit much too formal for a sunrise ceremony on the beach, he had a regal air about him that spoke of an upper-class background. I watched as he gazed out over the crowd, as if looking for someone in particular.

"Hi. My name is Kailani Pope." I held out my hand in greeting. "My friends call me Lani."

"Stuart Bronson." The man took my hand in return, although he didn't smile or alter his facial expression in any way. Although his presence on the beach indicated otherwise, he reminded me of a very formal butler in attendance at an English tea.

I glanced at Elva, who looked uncharacteristically tongue-tied. Elva was casual and outgoing and this very stoic man didn't seem at all like a good match for her, but as I've recently learned, the desires of the heart don't always match up with the logic of the mind.

"Elva mentioned the group had a new member," I continued. "I'm happy to have finally met you."

"I thought this was a senior group. You don't look a day over twenty-five."

"Twenty-four, actually. I'm sort of an honorary member because I'm usually free on Mondays to provide rides to those who need them, though I've been covering for one of the other water safety officers at the resort where I work the past couple of Mondays, which is why we haven't had a chance to meet."

"I see."

"Elva said you joined the group two weeks ago. Are you new to the island?"

"I moved here two months ago."

It occurred to me that two months was enough time for him to have picked up on the local custom of dressing down, but I didn't say as much. "How have you liked living on the island so far?"

"It's a much warmer climate than I'm used to."

"Yes, we have had a bit of a heat wave lately." The man didn't seem overly enthusiastic about the island or this conversation, which I guess I understood;

he appeared to be a fish out of water here. "Did you bring a shell for the ceremony?"

"No, I didn't." He looked around at the crowd. "I wasn't aware everyone would have one. I suppose I can just observe."

"No need. I have an extra shell in my Jeep. Wait here with Elva and I'll run to get it. She can show you how to use it."

Elva shot me a look of desperation as I turned and jogged away, but if she wanted to get to know Stuart Bronson she was going to have to talk to him at some point. Being given the task of teaching the newcomer a new skill seemed the perfect opening in my mind.

I was only gone for a few minutes, but by the time I returned Elva was standing alone. "Where did Stuart go?"

"I'm not sure." Elva looked around the crowd that had gathered at the waterline as the sky turned from gray to pink. "We were talking and then he got this odd look on his face. He said he needed to make a call and walked away. I haven't seen him since."

I looked toward the crowd. All the familiar faces seemed to be accounted for, but Stuart wasn't among the seniors gathered to wait. "He might have needed privacy for his call. Let's join the others.

I'm sure he'll be back before the sun actually peeks out over the horizon."

"I hope so. I'd hate for him to miss it."

I glanced at my watch. "It's just five forty-five. Sunrise isn't until five-fifty. I'm sure he'll rejoin us in plenty of time."

I wanted to ask Elva what exactly it was she saw in the man, but I knew that if I voiced my concern about his obvious lack of personality I'd come off sounding judgy, so I kept my thoughts to myself. At least for the time being. In all the time I'd known Elva, Stuart was the first man she'd shown any interest in, and I hated to say anything to interfere with that.

"You know, Janice has her eye on Stuart in spite of her rule about age," Elva informed me.

At seventy-four, Janice Furlong was one of the older members of the senior group that met for lunch before bingo on Mondays. For some reason after forty years of being a widow she'd decided she wanted to marry again. Not only had she signed up for a dating service but she knew exactly what she wanted in a man and wasn't going to waste her time with anyone else.

"Janice has her eye on pretty much every single male on the island under the age of fifty. Although Luke is too much of a southern gentleman to say anything, I'm sure she's been driving him crazy with the weekly list of chores she needs help with."

Luke Austin, a thirty-two-year-old friend, attends the senior events with me when his schedule allows, and Janice has made it clear he's just the type of cowboy she's after. Of course Luke is much too nice to turn Janice down when she calls to ask him for help with her rain gutters or furniture repair, so he ends up at her house at least one day a week for chores and a gourmet lunch.

"Janice is just messing around with Luke. She knows he'd never actually be interested in her as a potential wife, but Stuart—Stuart might just be interested in the package she's peddling."

"I wouldn't worry about it." I took Elva's hand. "Come on; the ceremony is starting."

Elva and I stood with the others as we joined together to welcome the sunrise on the longest day of the year. The sound of twenty-odd horns joined in harmony with the crashing waves for the two or three minutes it took the sun to rise in the sky brought tears to my eyes. I wished Luke could have been here, but his sister was visiting and he had taken her to one of the other islands for a couple of days.

When the ceremony was over everyone hugged one another as they wished them good health until the next solstice rolled around. There are some who think my desire to spend time with this particular group of friends strange, but there's something enlightening about spending time with people who have already lived the majority of their lives and are wiser for having done so.

"Will you be at lunch today?" Lucy Sanchez asked me.

"I will," I confirmed.

"And will Luke be there as well? I've been wanting to ask him about the flowerbed he promised to till."

I rolled my eyes. Janice wasn't the only member of the group who looked at Luke as a free source of labor, although most of the women who attended Monday lunch could well afford to pay someone to help out with their chores. But anyone they hired wasn't likely to fill out a pair of jeans or captivate them with their southern charm the way Luke did.

"I don't think Luke will be back on the island until later in the week."

Janice's smile faded. "That's too bad. He's missed the last two Mondays. I just assumed he hadn't come because you didn't. I hoped that now that you're back he would be too."

"He's had a lot of company from the mainland. I'm sure he'll join us next week."

"It seems to me that you ought to lasso that cowboy if you want to keep him for yourself," Elva whispered to Lani. "There aren't many men who bring to the table quite the package he does."

"I doubt either Janice or Lucy presents a risk to the future bliss you seem to imagine we're destined to share," I pointed out.

"Maybe not, but that new girl who's been boarding her horse at Luke's place is another thing entirely."

I frowned. Elva had a point. A friend of Luke's sister had recently moved to the island and he'd agreed to let her board her horse at his place. On the surface it seemed like an innocent enough arrangement. He had a horse ranch with plenty of room and she was a friend of the family. On the other hand, she was only a year younger than Luke, she knew his family and shared his past, and she was both single and drop-dead gorgeous. Maybe Janice Furlong didn't provide any competition to whatever sort of relationship Luke and I might develop, but Courtney Westlake most certainly might.

By the time we'd returned to the parking lot more than half the cars were gone. Elva looked around with a frown; Stuart's car was still in the lot and he had still to return. After a brief discussion I volunteered to take a look around for him. Elva was concerned that he might have taken the trail leading up to the bluff to get an enhanced view of the sunrise and slipped and fallen. The trail could be treacherous, which was why the seniors had decided to welcome the official start of summer from the beach below rather than making the climb.

I jogged almost every morning and surfed almost every day, so I was in pretty good shape and it didn't take me long to get back to the beach and up the steep trail. When I arrived at the top of the bluff I looked around but couldn't see anyone for as far as the eye could see. Then I looked out into the water and gasped. I quickly took off my sweatshirt and tennis shoes and dove off the edge of the bluff into the surf below.

"Did you see anyone in the area other than the members of your group?" my brother Jason, a detective for the Honolulu

Police Department, asked a couple of hours later, after the body had been recovered and everyone who was still in the area had been interviewed.

After I'd reached Stuart I swam his body to the beach and attempted CPR, but it was way too late, so I called 911 and informed a brokenhearted Elva that her crush had drowned. "No. No one. It was early, so it isn't as if the regular beach crowd had begun to arrive."

"And of the people who had gathered— did you notice anyone other than the victim walk away?"

"No, but to be honest I wasn't watching. After I met Stuart I went to my Jeep to get a second conch shell. When I returned Elva told me he'd stepped away to make a phone call. That was the last she saw of him."

"There are signs the victim struggled with his attacker. Did you hear anything?"

"With twenty-plus shells all raised in harmony at the same time?"

"Yeah, okay, I guess you wouldn't have heard a rocket take off." Jason ran his hand through his hair with a look of frustration on his face. "I can't believe I'm saying this, but I could use your help with this one."

"You can?" Color me shocked. Usually the first thing out of my older brother's mouth was to tell me to butt out and mind my own business.

"One of two things happened. Either the victim climbed up to the top of the bluff, got too close to the edge, and fell, or he climbed to the top of the bluff where he came into contact with a second person who helped him over the edge. Given the fact that the body shows signs of a struggle, right now I'm going to assume the second theory is the correct one. If Mr. Bronson was pushed from the ledge, I'm guessing one of the seniors in your group either killed him or saw something that can lead us to the killer. My men have been trying to interview everyone who's here, but the group as a whole has clammed up and I'm not sure why."

"Some of our seniors are the grumpy sort who, whatever the situation, just don't want to get involved. The problem is, once one person refuses to cooperate they all follow suit. I've seen it before. I really don't think it's anything personal; you just have to know how to talk to this particular group."

"Which is why I hoped you could talk to them. See what they know."

"You want me to interrogate the potential witnesses?" I clarified. The last time I'd interfered in a case Jason almost had torn me a new one.

"Not interrogate; just have a conversation with them. Friend to friend. Can you do that?"

I stood up and puffed out my chest like a proud cadet. "I'm on the case."

Jason rolled his eyes. "Remember, all I want you to do is to talk to these people. Nothing more. If you get a lead you're to call me right away."

"I know," I defended myself against his stern gaze. "I learned my lesson the last time."

Jason and his men returned to the bluff where they suspected the altercation had occurred to check for physical evidence and I helped Elva into my Jeep and drove her home. At first she was too upset even to consider going to the regular Monday lunch and bingo game, but when I kind of mentioned I was assisting the HPD with the case, she insisted on helping me help them.

The Monday lunch group usually consisted of seven or eight senior women, who, after they shared a meal, would all head over to the senior center for bingo.

I'd become an honorary member of the group when Elva broke her hip and was no longer able to drive, and Luke began attending as well after he'd met the women while helping me with a murder case the previous March.

The coffee shop at which the weekly group met was just a run-down diner that offered simple food in abundant quantities at reasonable prices. Because it was well off the beaten path, more often than not it was locals only who patronized the clean but shabby eatery. Coffee shop owner Wilma Goodwin was as loud and outspoken as she was ample, but she'd been a fixture in the area for so long that most people considered her presence as comforting as the food she whipped up every day.

"You didn't bring your handsome cowboy today?" Wilma asked, disappointment evident in her voice.

"Sorry. He's still out of town. I think he plans to join us for lunch next week."

"A finer-looking man I've never seen. You're one lucky gal to have lassoed that cowboy."

"I haven't *lassoed him*; we're just friends." I looked toward our regular table in the back, which was empty. "Have you heard from any of the others?"

"No, but you're a few minutes early, so I'm sure they'll be along shortly. Can I get you something to drink while you're waiting?"

"I'll have a Coke."

"Coffee for me," Elva added.

We settled into the booth and Elva took out a list and handed it to me.

"What's this?" I asked.

"A list of everyone at the sunrise ceremony this morning. I put a star next to the people who, as far as I know, have met Stuart."

There were nineteen people on the list because Elva hadn't bothered to list either of us. Of the nineteen, twelve were women and seven were men. Of the twelve women, six were members of the Monday lunch group and an additional four were regulars at bingo. Of the seven men, five attended bingo, which left two men and two women who, as far as Elva knew, had never had the opportunity to meet Stuart before that morning. Of course the four non-bingo-playing people attended other events that were sponsored by the senior center, so they might very well have met him at another time.

The odds of any of the seniors pushing Stuart off the bluff were slim. More than half of them wouldn't have the physical ability to climb the steep trail to the top, wrestle with a tall man, and push him to his death. But I hadn't seen anyone else in the area, so short of a senior as the killer, I had no suspects.

I put the list away as the others began to file in. Janice arrived with Beth Wasserman, a sixty-two-year-old woman who was in excellent health, who could very well have had the physical prowess to carry out the deed, although I had no idea what her motive might be. Janice had made it clear she had a thing for Stuart, and although she was the oldest in the lunch group, she also was in excellent health and could have both climbed to the top of the bluff and pushed the man from behind. I supposed if he'd spurned her advances she might have been angry enough to shove him.

The next to arrive were Connie Sullivan, Lucy Sanchez, and Diane Francis. All three of the women had been dealing with health issues lately that, in my opinion, would make it nearly impossible for them to be the killer. The only regular in our group who hadn't shown up was Susan Oberman, the youngest at the age of sixty, who very well could have the physical ability to climb the bluff and kill Stuart. Susan was married with four adult children. She wasn't a flirt like some of the others; based on her personality, I considered her the least likely to have a motive.

Everyone ordered and I turned the conversation to the events of the morning. While only two of the women at the table could have, in my opinion, even accessed the bluff, any one of the five could have seen something, so I began by asking that very question.

"I didn't see a single thing out of the ordinary," Connie began. "Of course I was one of the last to arrive other than you, Elva, and Stuart, but when I did get there everyone was standing around and talking and I didn't notice anyone acting oddly."

"Did you see Stuart go up to the bluff?" I wondered.

"No," Connie said, "though I really wasn't paying attention to either Stuart or the trail to the bluff. In fact I didn't even know Stuart was there until you all started asking if anyone had seen him."

"I saw him chatting with Dilly when he first arrived," Diane offered. Dilbert Portman—Dilly for short—was one of the men who played bingo and would have met Stuart.

"You know, now that I think about it, Dilly was none too happy when Stuart showed up at bingo that first time," Lucy provided. "It seemed as if he might have known him from somewhere else prior to his joining the group."

"It did seem as if the men might have been arguing," Diane agreed. "Not that I could hear what they were saying and not that I even paid all that much attention, but Dilly had a look on his face that most definitely wasn't a smile."

Having a chat with Dilly seemed like a good first step in my investigation. I just hoped he would attend bingo today.

"Which of you was the first to arrive at the beach?" I asked.

The women all looked at one another. "I guess of the six of us I was," Beth answered. "I was the third overall, after Cliff Wells and Greg Collins."

Greg could barely walk, so I didn't consider him a suspect, although he might have seen someone in the area early on. Cliff was a hot head who had a temper and the physical ability to follow through and kill someone. Again, I had no idea what sort of motive he might have, but as far as I was concerned he was on my suspect list until cleared. The main problem with interviewing Cliff was that he didn't play bingo; I'd have to track him down some other way.

Although Janice and Beth had the ability to climb up to the bluff, they both said they were together the entire time once Janice arrived, so I crossed them off my list, along with the seniors I felt were physically unable to have killed Stuart. By the end of lunch I had two lists: those who physically could have done it and hadn't been cleared for any other reason and those who didn't but I still needed to speak to. On list one I had: Susan Oberman, who hadn't shown up for lunch; Dilbert Portman, who'd been seen talking to Stuart; Cliff Wells, who had a bad temper; Franny Littleton, who wasn't a member of the lunch group but was in excellent shape and played bingo and so would have known Stuart; and Sam Riverton, who was a member of the bingo group and no one remembered talking to that day.

On list number two—the list of people who couldn't have done it but might know something about it—I had Olivia Steadman, Greg Collins, and Regina Evans. Luckily, all three should be at bingo.

"So what do you think?" Elva asked as we drove from the coffee shop to the senior center, where bingo was held.

"I'm not sure," I said. "I hate to think any of the seniors would do such an awful thing, but no one remembers seeing anyone else around. It's possible the killer was already up on the bluff before any of us arrived."

"It does seem odd that none of the gals remembered seeing Stuart go up to the bluff," Elva added.

"Yeah, although everyone was looking out at the horizon as we waited for the sun, and the trail to the bluff is behind where we were standing. I suppose unless they turned around those of us on the beach wouldn't have seen Stuart. Although you were between Stuart and the trail. Don't you remember seeing him go in that direction?"

Elva shook her head. "I watched him walk away, but he headed in the other direction. I saw him disappear behind those bushes that grow along the south end of the beach, where the coastline curves. Once he reached the curve he would have been out of view, but it does make sense he would have had to double back to climb up to the bluff. I have no idea why he would do such a thing. He certainly wasn't dressed for a hike."

No, he wasn't, although he wasn't dressed for the beach either. "What do you really know about Stuart?" I asked as I turned off the highway onto the side street where the senior center was located.

"Not a lot," Edna admitted. "We never talked except for very cursory conversations at bingo."

"And yet it seems you really liked the guy."

Elva blushed and looked away. "He had a look about him. He reminded me of a man I dated a long time ago, before I married or even moved to the island. I guess you could say I've always wondered how my life would have turned out if I'd taken a different path and married him. Of course Steve was a bit more outgoing than Stuart, and he smiled a lot more often. But the height and general build are very similar and Steve tended to take time with his appearance and dress sharply no matter the occasion, as did Stuart."

I pulled into the parking lot of the senior center. "Did you stay in touch with Steve?"

"No. We both got married and we went our separate ways. I really hadn't thought about him much at all during the ensuing years until Stuart showed up, reigniting long-buried feelings."

"Maybe you should look this Steve up," I suggested as I chose a parking space. "It's been a lot of years. You're currently single; maybe he is as well."

Elva smiled. "Thanks, but I think I'll stick with my memories. The real thing could never be as good. So how do you want to play this when we get inside?"

"I guess we'll just see who's here and try to strike up conversations with those we can. If nothing else, maybe some of the seniors on my list will alibi one another the way Janice and Beth did."

The first suspect I ran into upon entering the senior center was Olivia Steadman, a retired teacher who suffered from back issues, which was why I was certain she couldn't have hiked up the bluff trail and pushed Stuart into the surf below. She was the observant sort, though, so I hoped she might have seen something that would lead me to the person who had helped Stuart to his untimely death.

"Afternoon, Olivia," I greeted her. "That sure was a moving ceremony this morning."

"Wasn't it? When the horns all joined in harmony to welcome the summer sun I got chills down my spine."

"It was really beautiful, although what happened next was less than beautiful. I guess you heard about Stuart."

"I left before you discovered his body, but I heard about it the minute I got here. The poor man. Who would do such a thing?"

"Do you remember seeing him at the ceremony this morning?"

"I saw him speaking to you and Elva, but the only reason I even noticed that was because I had been chatting with Dilly, and right in the middle of my story about the MRI I have scheduled for next week he frowned and then wandered off."

"He wandered off? Did you see where he went?"

"He walked toward the spot where you all were talking, but only a few steps in that direction, before changing course and heading over to speak to Cliff."

"And after that?"

"I don't know. The sun was starting to come up, so I turned my attention to the horizon."

"Do you happen to remember seeing Sam Riverton during the ceremony?" So far no one I'd spoken to had remembered seeing him, but I knew he'd been at the beach that morning.

"Sure, I remember seeing Sam. He was toward the back of the pack, talking to Susan Oberman. By the way, have you seen Susan? She was supposed to stop by my place and drop off some items she wants to donate for the rummage sale, but she never came by and she isn't answering her phone."

I frowned. "No, I haven't seen her, and she didn't come to lunch as planned. I hope she's okay."

Olivia shrugged. "I'm sure she is. She does tend to be forgetful at times. It looks like Regina just arrived. I need to ask her about the items she plans to donate. I hope you figure out who killed that poor man."

"Yeah," I said as Olivia walked away, "me too."

# Chapter 2

When Elva and I got home from bingo I did as I'd promised and called my detective brother Jason. The last time there had been a murder in our area, I'd tried to best him and solve the murder before he could, but in the end my need to compete almost had gotten me killed. This time, I decided, I'd do as I was asked and leave the rest to the pros.

"I've managed to whittle the list of twenty seniors down to four people you might want to speak to," I informed him. "Susan Oberman was at the sunrise ceremony this morning but didn't show up for either our weekly lunch or bingo. I went by her house, but there was no one home, and I've left three messages on her cell, but she hasn't called me back. On the surface I don't see how she would have a motive to kill Stuart, but she's in good shape physically, so she could have done it. I'll text you her contact information."

"Okay," Jason answered. "Who else?"

"Stuart was seen speaking to Dilbert Portman. Several people mentioned that Dilly and Stuart didn't get along and that they seemed to have known each other prior to Stuart joining the bingo group. Dilly didn't show up for bingo either. I don't know where he lives and I don't have a phone number for him; other than bingo, I don't really know him."

I could hear Jason writing. At least he was taking the intel I'd gathered seriously, which was a first. "Cliff Wells was at the ceremony this morning. He doesn't play bingo and I don't know him well at all, but I have witnessed that he seems to have a quick temper. He was the first person to arrive at the ceremony this morning, so if there was some sort of setup he could have been in on it, and there wouldn't have been anyone around to see what he was doing."

"Do you have his contact information?"

"No, but I'm pretty sure Greg Collins does. I'll text you his phone number."

"Okay, that's three. Who's the fourth?"

"Franny Littleton was also at the ceremony this morning but wasn't at bingo, although she usually is. I have no specific reason to suspect her except for the fact that no one remembered her being with the group once the sun began to rise. Franny's a nice woman and I can't imagine she'd kill anyone, but she certainly is physically capable of doing so.

I'll text you her contact information as well."

"Anyone else?"

"No, that's it. Everyone else remembered standing with someone else during the ceremony who likewise verified the alibi of the other person. I spoke to everyone other than those I've just listed and no one remembers seeing a stranger in the area, nor do they remember seeing Stuart go up to the bluff. Of course, everyone's attention was fully on the horizon once the sun began to come up and the trail to the bluff was behind where everyone was standing."

"Okay. Thanks, little sis. It looks like you've done an excellent job weeding down the list. The team and I will take it from here."

"Okay. Will I see you at dinner on Sunday?"

"I should be there unless this case totally blows up."

"I'm sure you and your team will have it wrapped up in no time," I offered just before hanging up. I really wanted to stay in my brother's good graces, but there was a part of me that hated to simply walk away from a case I felt so connected to.

"So, are you really going to stay out of it?" My roommate, cousin, and best friend,

Kekoa, asked when I joined her on the lanai.

"I really am. Jason has just started to trust me again after the last time I tried to interfere in his case and I don't want to ruin the progress I've made."

"Even though you aren't officially investigating, do you have a feel for who might be guilty?"

I thought about it. None of the seniors still on the list were obvious suspects, but I supposed if I had to, I'd put my money on Dilly. If the rumor was true that they knew each other prior to Stuart joining the seniors, Dilly could have a motive that was related to something in the past that no one else knew anything about. I told Kekoa as much and then asked for her opinion based on what I'd shared. She thought it was odd that Susan hadn't shown up for lunch or bingo, even though she'd mentioned to several of the others that she planned to be there. Susan didn't seem like the killing kind, but her behavior had been odd. She was usually pretty dependable—the type to call to let someone know if her plans changed.

Kekoa and I batted around a few additional ideas before we both agreed that without a lot more information we were pretty much at a dead end.

"I'm thinking about heading out and tracking down some waves. Do you want to come?" I asked. Although we lived right on the water, the waves near our condo weren't always the best for surfing.

"Actually, Sean and Kevin are back from Europe and have invited everyone over for dinner." Sean Trainor and Kevin Green were flight attendants who were away more than they were home, but when they were at the condos, they were usually up for throwing a party.

"Sounds like fun. I'll just take Sandy for a run, then, and come back to get cleaned up." I called my golden lab to my side and headed out the door.

Kekoa and I had a third roommate: Cameron Carrington, Cam for short. We lived in unit one of Shell Beach Condominiums, a six-unit complex. Elva lived next door in unit two, and next to her, in unit three, lived a teacher named Mary and her adopted daughter, Malia. Carina West, a hula dancer for one of the resorts, lived in unit four, and Sean and Kevin had unit five. Until two months earlier, unit six had been occupied by a tenant everyone knew as Mr. B but had turned out to be an Interpol agent named Mallari Baldini. Mallari had been on the island to investigate two situations, one of which was her suspicion that Sean and Kevin were international thieves and smugglers. While she was never able to prove their guilt, she was unable to establish their innocence either. After an unsuccessful attempt to gain the evidence she needed, Mallari had left the island and a new tenant, a surfer, who went by the name Shredder, had moved into unit 6.

Shredder was an interesting guy. On the surface he appeared to have no means of support, yet he was able to pay for a condo on the beach that wasn't cheap. He'd never really said where he was from, and if you asked him, he was apt to reply with something vague, such as *here and there*. He surfed every day, even when the weather was bad, and otherwise lived very simply. Most evenings you could find him on the lanai playing his ukulele, and other than a dog named Riptide, who was constantly by his side, he didn't appear to have any family or friends. At least not any on the island.

I estimated Shredder was about our age—in his midtwenties—although he'd never said as much. He had the classic surfer boy look: bleached blond hair, a deep golden tan, big brown eyes, and not an ounce of fat anywhere on his body. I was sure he could have any number of girls on the island, but as far as I could tell, he preferred Riptide's company.

Riptide, a Border collie mix with tons of energy, was an amazing dog. He could not only swim but surf. Not by himself of course, but more often than not if Shredder was riding a wave you'd see Riptide on the board in front of him. Shredder and the dog tended to attract quite a bit of attention, though as far as I could tell neither of them were all that interested in interacting with the crowd that gathered to watch them. Despite their solitary natures, both Shredder and Rip fit right in with the condo family, seeming glad to have the companionship we provided.

Cam was home from work by the time I returned from my run and, after I showered and cleaned up, the three of us, along with Sandy, walked down to Sean and Kevin's apartment. When we arrived Sean was showing Carina a vase he'd picked up on his travels.

"That's beautiful," I commented. "It looks Japanese."

"It is. A very expensive antique."

"And you got it in France?"

"Tokyo."

I frowned. "I thought you were going to France and Italy."

"I did, but I had some downtime, so I took a little side trip."

Japan seemed like more than a little side trip from Italy, but I didn't say anything. I hated that the Interpol agent had put it in my head that Sean and Kevin might be thieves. Now any time they did anything that seemed even a tiny bit suspicious I wondered about their actions. I knew Sean's father had been a thief who had shown Sean the tricks of the trade; he freely admitted as much. Could these friendly men who felt like family really be international criminals, as Baldini suspected?

"It's a beautiful vase, but it doesn't go with your décor," I said.

Sean has an eye for style and design and the vase, which was painted in shades of orange and red, didn't look at all like something he would add to the condo, which was beautifully decorated in shades of gray, blue, and white to match the sand and the sea.

"It's actually for a friend," Sean answered.

A friend? As in a client you procured a piece of artwork for? Geez, I really did need to get this whole smuggling ring thing out of my mind. Sean was a nice guy and a good friend. Sure, he'd grown up in a family of thieves and certainly had the skills to pull off at least low-key heists, but he was also a hard worker who cared about others. I absolutely refused to think the worst of him and yet, as I glanced across the room at Kevin, who was chatting with Cam, I couldn't help but wonder. I'm sure as senior flight attendants Sean and Kevin made descent money, but the condo they shared was expertly decorated and outfitted with expensive furniture and top-of-the-line electronics. Additionally, they both drove really nice cars. I guess one couldn't help but wonder.

"Sean," Malia yelled as she came in with Mary and propelled herself across the room and into Sean's arms. Luckily, Carina interpreted what was about to happen and took the vase out of Sean's hands.

"I've missed you," he exclaimed as he hugged her.

"I missed you too."

Carina handed the vase to Kevin, who put it away in a hard-to-reach cabinet over the refrigerator.

"Malia has been so excited that you were finally coming home," Mary announced as Malia crossed the room to hug Kevin while Sean hugged Mary.

When Mary and Malia had first come to look at the condo in which they now lived Elva had informed me that the pair would fit in perfectly with our little family, and she couldn't have been more right. While we all enjoyed having a child on the property, Sean and Kevin seemed to glow when she was around. In return, Malia seemed to have adopted them as surrogate fathers.

"Is Shredder coming?" Mary asked.

"Yeah," Kevin answered. "He's surfing, but he should be here soon."

"Elva stuck her head out her door as Malia and I left our condo and said she'd be here in a few minutes," Mary informed everyone.

I loved it when the family all came together. In all, there were ten people and two dogs living at the Shell Beach complex, and every one of them meant almost as much to me as my real family.

"So, tell us about this new murder investigation you've become involved in." Kevin looked toward me as I grabbed a soda from the fridge.

I walked across the cool tile floor in my bare feet as I twisted the cap from the bottle and took a quick drink before answering. "I wouldn't say I'm really involved, although I *was* the one to find the body and I *have* spent most of the day talking to people about it. It's my guess it's going to be a difficult case to solve, although on the surface the suspect pool seems pretty limited."

"I hadn't heard someone died." Mary looked surprised. "Who was it?"

"A friend of Elva's from her senior group." I took the next couple of minutes to fill everyone in.

"Wow, that's really tragic," Mary murmured.

"Elva's having a hard time with the whole thing, which can be understood," I informed the others. "It might be best not to bring it up unless she does."

"Will Luke be joining us this evening?" Carina asked.

"He's still off the island. The last I heard, he hoped to be back by the end of the week."

"Good; then he can help you with the investigation."

"I'm not investigating," I insisted.

I couldn't be certain, but it seemed as if everyone in the room had joined together for a coordinated eye roll. I guess I couldn't blame them. I do have a natural curiosity and a slight tendency to follow that curiosity into dangerous situations. Some call me impulsive and irresponsible, but I like to think I'm more inquisitive and spontaneous. After my last attempt to investigate a murder on my own and the near-disastrous results, I liked to think I'd turned over a new leaf.

"I brought beer," Shredder said as he entered the condo.

"The refrigerator is full, but there's room in the bucket," Sean instructed. The guys had filled a large tub with ice that they were using to keep a variety of drinks cool.

"How was the surfing?" I asked.

"Gnarly. You should have come."

"It was late by the time I got back from bingo."

"I thought bingo was over at two."

"It ran late today because I spent some time interviewing everyone about the murder at the sunrise ceremony this morning."

"There was a murder? Who died?"

"A man named Stuart Bronson."

Shredder got a strange look on his face. It only lasted a second before he changed his expression, but it was long enough for me to notice.

"Did you know him?" I asked.

Shredder hesitated. "No. Never heard of him. Was he a member of the senior group?"

"I guess. I hadn't met him until today and no one seemed to be talking to him while I was there, but Elva said he'd joined the senior center a few weeks ago."

"Bummer. So what are we grilling tonight?"

On one hand I had no idea how Shredder could be connected to someone like Stuart, but the fact that he'd changed the topic so quickly made me suspicious. Stuart had said he'd moved to the island two months ago, which was just about the same time Shredder had shown up at the condominiums. Could the two men have a connection none of us knew about? I could see Shredder didn't want to talk about Stuart and Elva had just walked in, so I didn't want to push it, but when it was time for Riptide to go out to do his business, Sandy and I would head out for a break as well.

We BBQ'd the steaks Sean and Kevin provided and ate the side dishes everyone else brought, and then Shredder and I headed out to take the two dogs for a walk. I think Sandy was happy to have another dog in the building. Shredder would stop by to grab Sandy when he took Riptide out even if I wasn't home or was unable to join them, so Sandy was getting a lot of extra outdoor time.

"It looks like it's going to be a gorgeous sunset," I said conversationally. I figured it was bad form to jump right into an accusation that I thought he knew more about Stuart than he was letting on.

"What is it you're really after?"

"What makes you think I'm after anything?"

Shredder stopped walking and looked toward the setting sun. "Because the sunset looks to be average at best and in all the time I've known you, you've never once mentioned the sunset even when it actually was spectacular."

I noticed two things. One was that Shredder suddenly appeared to be a lot more observant than he usually was, and the second was that he'd lost his surfer boy accent.

"Very well; if you must know what's on my mind, I noticed your expression when I mentioned Stuart."

"What expression?"

"A combination of recognition and surprise. Maybe even a little alarm thrown in. You covered it up right away, but still, I'm curious about what it meant and why you covered it up."

I noticed small frown lines around Shredder's eyes. Maybe he wasn't as young as I'd assumed. He was in great shape and you'd have to be completely blind not to appreciate his long blond hair and killer physique, but suddenly he didn't seem so much a carefree kid as a middle-aged man running from life.

"You know, when I first met you, I could tell your tendency to notice every little thing was going to get me into trouble."

"Are you? In trouble?"

"Not really. It's more that I've worked hard to disappear and I really prefer not to be found."

"Disappear from where? Or what?"

Shredder looked toward the dogs romping in the waves. He had a look on his face that could only be described as weariness.

"You can tell me what's going on," I encouraged. "I can keep a secret."

"I'm sure you can, but every time I let someone in just a tiny bit I put both them and myself in danger."

"Are you running from the law?"

"No. I'm not a fugitive."

"An ex-wife? A disgruntled employer? The mob?"

Shredder started walking. He didn't indicate whether he wanted me to follow, but I made the decision and filed in beside him. We walked in total silence for about five minutes until he stopped and looked out at the calm sea.

"I know it may appear that I've lived my life as a free spirit and don't have a care in the world, but the truth of the matter is that not so long ago I had a job, a family, and a fiancée."

"So what happened to them?"

"Five years ago, shortly after my twenty-eighth birthday, I was working late when I heard sounds coming from down the hall. I worked at an investment bank and it wasn't all that unusual for there to be other employees on the premises after-hours, so at first I ignored it. Then I heard what sounded like a suppressed scream, and I decided I'd better go investigate. I found my boss dead on the floor of his office. Someone had slit his throat."

"Oh, God. What did you do?"

"I called 911 and waited for the police to arrive. They took the body away, then took me down to the station for questioning. At first they thought I might have done it. The truth was, my boss and I didn't get along and I didn't have an alibi. After a few days the detective in charge found some evidence that the leader of one of the gangs in the area was using our firm to launder money, and the police believed my boss was in the middle of the whole thing. The problem was, they didn't have any more proof this gang leader was involved in the murder than they had that I was. For a while we were both considered to be suspects, but then some new evidence turned up that seemed to point at me as the killer. I knew the *proof* they'd found was bogus; I was being framed."

"So you ran off when it looked like you might go to jail?"

"No. The detective I was working with believed I was innocent despite the evidence to the contrary, so he set up a sting to try to prove the gang leader was guilty of the money laundering, my boss's murder, or both. In the end it turned out the gang leader was being framed by a dirty cop."

I narrowed my gaze. The story Shredder had just told me sounded familiar. Too familiar.

"You're lying," I accused him.

Shredder looked surprised. "Why do you think that?"

"Because the story you just told me was the plot of a movie Carina and I watched a few weeks ago."

Shredder shrugged. "I guess I'm busted."

"So what's your real story? Why lie?"

"You seemed determined to uncover my dark, mysterious past, and based on what I've observed about you over the past few months you're like a dog with a bone when you get an idea in your head. So I gave you a story. It might not be true, but admit it: I had you going for a while. Where did I lose you?"

"A cop as the bad guy. I hate stories where the cop turns out to be the bad guy, so they tend to stick with me."

"Damn. I should have thought about that and stopped while I was ahead."

"So what's the real story?" I repeated.

"I don't have one. I don't know Stuart, and any expression you think you might have seen is completely in your mind."

I paused and looked at Shredder. "Look, I get that you're entitled to your own secrets and I know we've only known each other for a short time, but you can trust me. If you're in some sort of trouble you can tell me."

Shredder smiled. "I know. I've been around you enough to realize that you'll do anything for your family, and I know you consider the residents at Shell Beach to be family. But I really don't have any deep, dark secret. I'm just a guy who likes to live in the present and doesn't want to complicate things by hanging on to the past."

Fat chance that was the truth. I wasn't sure what Shredder was hiding, but I was determined to found out.

# Chapter 3

## Monday June 27

It was a week since I'd found Stuart floating in the water. A week of struggling to keep my promise to my brother to stay out of things; a week of quelling my natural inclination to jump into the investigation and test the theories that had been rambling around in my mind.

I knew Stuart's death would still be the main topic of conversation at the regular Monday lunch today, and the women with whom I'd dine would expect me to provide some sort of an update. The only thing I knew for certain was that apparently, no one had seen anything, and everyone who had been interviewed seemed to have an alibi, or so they said. Jason had admitted that several of those alibis were soft as best.

After a quick run with Sandy I showered and dressed in a new sundress. I'd made the decision to dress up a bit for the weekly event, not because Luke was finally home and I was going to see him for the first time in almost two weeks but because the dress was a sunny yellow that I hoped would bring an element of joy to an event I imagined could turn out to be quite depressing. I knew Elva was hoping I'd agree to secretly look into things because Jason and his team seemed to be getting nowhere, and there was a part of me that, like Elva, was tired of waiting for the answers everyone hoped would explain such a tragedy.

"Don't you look nice," Elva said when I knocked on her door. "I take it this means Luke will be joining us for lunch today."

"Don't make a big deal. It's going to be a warm afternoon and this dress is comfortable."

Elva put her hands up in surrender. "Not making a big deal, just paying you a compliment. Yellow really is your color, and it's a difficult one to pull off. Me, if I wear yellow, whatever the shade, I tend to look washed out and pasty."

"You have that yellow and white blouse I really like," I pointed out.

"I suppose the bright yellow contrasting with the white is the exception. Perhaps I should change and then we can match."

"No, you look great already. I've always loved that shade of green on you. Besides, we need to get going or we'll be late. By the way, do you know why lunch was moved up an hour? Ten seems early for lunch."

"I'm not sure. We can ask the girls when we get there."

Elva diverted her eyes, which led me to believe she knew more than she was saying, but I let it go because I'd learn the answer to my question soon enough. "Did you remember to bring the crochet pattern Lucy wanted to borrow?"

"It's in my bag. I was hoping we could stop to pick up some new yarn after bingo. I want to make a crib blanket for Janice's new great-granddaughter."

"I heard her oldest granddaughter had had another baby. Boy or girl?"

"Girl. And such a cutie. Luckily, she takes after her mother and seems to have been spared her daddy's big nose."

"Janice's grandson-in-law doesn't have a big nose."

"Yes, he does. Of course he has those big beautiful eyes that help to balance his face out a bit."

I thought it odd that Elva had paid so much attention to the physical characteristics of the baby's father but decided to change the subject and brought up the blanket Elva had crocheted for Malia. She'd really put a lot of work into it and Malia had been thrilled with the effort.

I helped Elva into my Jeep, then pulled out of the drive and headed into town. I had a feeling our Monday lunch was going to be well attended thanks to the continuing speculation about Stuart's murder. I mean, what good was it to have a theory if you didn't have someone to share it with? I know most of the seniors would assume I had some solid leads after the way I solved the murder of a developer a few months back, although I had to admit I really hadn't solved the case so much as stumbled onto the killer quite by accident.

I pulled into the parking lot of the coffee shop and parked next to Luke, who was waiting for me. He pulled me into a bear hug as soon I got out and told me how much he'd missed me. It had been a while since we'd been able to hang out together, and while it wasn't so long ago that I'd considered him my mortal enemy, I found I'd missed him as much as he professed to have missed me.

"So how was Maui?" I asked after Luke helped Elva down from the Jeep and gifted her with her own Luke Austin special hug.

"It was nice."

"You don't sound sure."

"It was nice, but as much as I love my family, I find I'm more than ready for the end of my visits with them. It's a lot of work entertaining everyone all the time. It'll be good to get back to a regular routine."

The minute we walked into the diner the women who were already there descended on Luke. Four seniors had arrived early. Janice was sitting at the head of the table and seemed to have been leading a discussion that had ended the moment we walked in. Sitting to Janice's right were regulars Diane and Beth, and to her left was a woman I had only met a few times, Emmy Jean Thornton.

"There's my cowboy," Wilma Goodwin exclaimed as she waddled over to Luke and demanded he give her some sugar.

Luke hugged Wilma and politely greeted each woman in turn, making sure a hug was returned with a hug and a kiss to the cheek returned with the same. There weren't many men who would be so gracious to a group of women twice his age. By the time our drinks were served Luke had a long list of honey do's from the senior honeys in his life.

Once all the women had gotten their fill of attention from their cowboy, the topic of conversation moved from rain gutters to murder. It seemed this small contingent of senior women had gathered early specifically for the purpose of discussing the situation. If the head nods were any indication, it seemed Janice spoke for all of them when she announced that they were tired of waiting for answers and had decided to help.

"You're all going to investigate?" I confirmed.

"We are," Janice answered. "And because we don't have all the resources you and Luke have, we hoped both of you would be willing to help us."

"Help you do what exactly?"

"Find the killer."

I looked around at the women and finally understood why my brothers felt the need to protect me. I could see they were serious and I knew they felt they could help, but the last thing I wanted was for any of them to get hurt. I realized many of these women were in decent shape physically, but the youngest of them was sixty, with the ages spiraling upward from there. I was about to suggest that perhaps they might want to take a step back and let the younger generation handle the investigation, but then I realized that would make them feel belittled because of their age just the way I did when my brothers tried to tell me to stick to the sidelines because of my gender or my size. I looked at Luke, who simply shrugged. Fat lot of help he was.

"I get why you're growing impatient, but Janice, you have that new granddaughter I'm sure you want to spend time with, and Beth, you have a husband and kids to think about. Investigating could be dangerous."

"We've got our minds and our wits and most of us still have our original body parts," Janice answered.

"What about Diane's new hip?" I asked.

"Doesn't slow her down any more than Emmy Jean's new boobs," Janice pointed out.

I glanced at Emmy Jean, who only attended senior events sporadically, and it did appear she'd had a boob job. She worked on herself more often than any woman I'd ever met. She was one of the younger group members at sixty-two, but already she'd had a face-lift, a tummy tuck, and now new boobs to round out the package.

"Maybe we can discuss your ideas and then Luke and I can check some things out and get back to you," I suggested.

"The girls and I want in on the action," Emmy Jean insisted.

I wasn't sure if Emmy Jean was referring to her fellow seniors or her new boobs when she mentioned *the girls*, but either way I could see the women at the table had made up their minds. I momentarily considered another attempt at talking them out of it, but based on the determination in their faces, I'd most likely be unsuccessful. While I preferred they didn't get involved at all, I certainly wasn't going to let them investigate on their own. I looked at Luke with an expression that I hoped communicated that I needed his help with this.

Based on his next comment, he either didn't understand or didn't agree. "I think if the ladies want to help we should let them, although I'm not sure this is the best venue for discussing the matter. What do you say we all meet at my house later this afternoon for a BBQ and strategy session?"

Luke's announcement was met with applause from everyone present. I wished I could say I was equally thrilled, but I couldn't help but wonder if this whole thing would end badly.

By the time I arrived at Luke's with Sandy, the women—other than Elva, who was with me—were already there. Luke was busy behind the outdoor bar mixing up a pitcher of frozen drinks, while the others were lounging around the pool. Janice and Diane were sitting at a table under an umbrella chatting, while Beth, the fitness buff of the bunch, was doing laps, and Emmy Jean was showing off her surgically enhanced body sunbathing in the tiniest bikini I'd ever seen.

"Can I get you ladies a drink?" Luke asked when Elva and I walked up.

"Do you have anything nonalcoholic?" Elva asked.

"How about a virgin daiquiri?"

"Sounds perfect."

"Strawberry or lime?"

"Strawberry, please."

Luke blended the daiquiri for Elva and then set to mixing up a margarita for me.

"So how are we going to play this?" I asked Luke after Elva joined Janice and Diane in the shade.

"Play it?"

"We can't have them running around putting themselves in danger. I know they want to help, but Diane and Elva barely have a pair of workable legs between them."

Luke handed me the cold, frosty drink before answering. "The women want to help. It's my sense they plan to do so whether we work with them or not. The best way to keep them safe is to control the investigation. I don't have all the details because I've been away, but I'm sure we can find safe yet helpful tasks for them to perform."

"Yeah, okay." I took a sip of my frozen drink. "That sounds like a good idea."

"I've missed you," Luke whispered.

"Shh. The others will hear."

"They won't hear, and even if they did, is there a problem with my missing you? I haven't seen you in over two weeks."

"I'm just not ready for us to be a couple yet. At least not in public."

Luke leaned in so his lips brushed my ear as he spoke. "So later, when we're alone?"

I couldn't help but smile. Luke and I had been dancing around the whole relationship issue for months. After a rocky start we'd settled into a friendship that, to be honest, I'd been dead set against in the beginning. I was a native Hawaiian with deep roots in the islands and he was a displaced cowboy who would surely grow tired of island life after a while and return to the huge state of Texas, where he'd grown up. I knew in my heart he would never be happy with island life in the long run with the same conviction that

I knew I would never be happy anywhere else. Still, Luke had made it clear he was interested in taking our friendship to the next level, and I was tempted, even if it was doomed to lead to heartbreak and discontent.

"Elva rode with me, so I'll need to leave when she does," I finally answered. "I have to work tomorrow, but maybe we can hang out after."

"Or," Luke countered, "maybe I can follow you to your place so you can drop Elva off and then I can bring you back here for a swim? I'm sure the seniors won't stay long."

I hesitated.

"It's just a swim," he said encouragingly.

"I guess a swim would be nice."

Luke smiled and took a step back. "Okay, then let's get this meeting started. I thought we'd chat first and then I'd grill some kebabs to go with the salad I threw together when I got home. I even have crusty bread fresh from the bakery."

"Have you always been such a Suzy Homemaker?"

Luke's eyes sparkled when he grinned. "Always."

God, I wanted to kiss those lips. Maybe an agreement to date casually wouldn't be so bad. On the other hand, I wasn't sure anything I did with Luke would end up being casual.

"My brother's managed to clear all but two of the seniors who attended the sunrise ceremony," I began once we were all seated around the table with our drinks. The sound of the waterfall in the background lent a relaxing feel to what would otherwise be, I predicted, a stressful conversation.

"Which two?" Elva asked.

"Susan and Dilly. While I have no reason to suspect either of them, Dilly has been unwilling to explain his whereabouts after the ceremony and Susan hasn't returned any of his calls."

"Does that matter?" Diane asked. "I mean, Stuart was already dead. What difference does it make what they did afterward?"

"Both Susan and Dilly left the ceremony immediately after sunrise. Elva and I stayed to chat with a few people, so it was a good twenty minutes later that I found the body. My brother feels it's possible someone who left the ceremony early could have killed Stuart between the time they left and I found the body. Neither Susan nor Dilly came to bingo that day and neither have provided alibis. I think it would be beneficial if one of you had a chat with them, friend to friend."

"I'll take Dilly," Emmy Jean offered. "The guy's been eyeing the girls ever since I showed up to our monthly potluck with them. I can get him to talk."

"Great. And who wants to talk to Susan?"

"Diane and I can do it," Beth volunteered. "We have that healthy eating class together."

"What about me?" Janice asked. "I may not have Emmy Jean's boobs, but I can talk a man out of whatever secrets he might have."

"I have a feeling Cliff knows something, although he did have an alibi for where he went after the ceremony, so it doesn't look like he's guilty of killing Stuart. Maybe you can find out what he knows and who he might be covering for."

"You know, it just occurred to me that maybe Stuart getting whacked had something to do with the reason he came to the island in the first place," Janice added.

"You know why he came to the island?"

"Of course. I had him checked out before I made the decision to pursue such an old man."

"He was younger than you," Elva pointed out.

"Perhaps, but he was still quite a bit out of my age range in terms of a love interest."

"What did you find out?" I asked, trying to get the women focused on the murder and not their rivalry.

"Shortly after I met Stuart, I ran into him at a restaurant in town. You know how I like to take control of a potential relationship right up-front, so when I saw him I sashayed over to his table and asked if I could join him. I think he was going to decline, but I'm not one to take no for an answer, so I sat myself down and ordered us a bottle of wine. The good stuff. Anyway, as I was saying, I was trying to decide whether the man possessed enough assets to make an exception to my predetermined age range, so I started off by asking him about his career. I assumed, given the fact that he always wears a suit, that he was some sort of a businessman, but he informed me that he worked in private security."

"Security? As in a security guard?" I asked.

"So it would seem, but I got the feeling it was more than that. If I had to guess he was some sort of a bodyguard."

"He seemed a little old to be a bodyguard," I said.

"Perhaps, but I still think his job entailed protecting a person rather than an object. Anyway, he was pretty tight-lipped but not all that good at holding his liquor, so I got him loosened up and he finally told me he was on the island to retrieve something."

"Like what?" Elva asked.

I could tell Elva was green with envy that Janice had actually dined with the man she had only worked up the courage to admire from afar, but, like the rest of us, she couldn't help but be drawn into the story.

"I don't know. Despite the amount of alcohol I managed to get into him, he wouldn't say anything more than that, and it was clear he was sorry he'd said as much as he had. It's occurred to me that perhaps whatever he was after is what got him killed."

"That makes sense. Why haven't you mentioned this to anyone before?"

Janice shrugged. "It slipped my mind."

I didn't buy that for a minute. Janice was as sharp as a tack. It was my guess that she'd been waiting for Luke to return so she could provide a relevant piece of information directly to the cowboy she was obviously crushing on.

"Do any of you know how Stuart got involved with the seniors?" I asked. "He mentioned to me that he moved here two months ago, but as far as I know he only joined the group a few weeks ago."

The women all looked at one another. It was evident none of them knew for certain, but they all supposed he'd met one of the other seniors somewhere and that person had told him about the activities at the senior center.

"Someone said Dilly seemed to know him before he attended his first senior event."

"Yes, but Dilly seemed surprised to find him there," Janice insisted. "It didn't seem as if he'd been the one to invite him."

"I suppose we can ask around," Beth suggested.

"Maybe we should all venture out to gather information and then meet back here," Emmy Jean suggested. "Say in a day or two around the cocktail hour?"

"I'm working until seven the next two days," I informed them.

"And I'm usually in bed by nine," Diane shared.

"How about Luke here acting as the point person for this?" Emmy Jean said, angling her body toward him in a way that couldn't help but show off her enhanced assets. "If we get a lead we'll call him and he can organize the next meeting."

Poor Luke. I had a feeling the women from the senior center were going to drive him crazy with phone calls whether they had leads or not.

# Chapter 4

## Tuesday, June 28

I loved my job as a water safety officer (WSO) for the Dolphin Bay Resort. At least most of the time. Today was hot and muggy and I'd been assigned to the family pool, which was by far my least favorite place, though even with this gig you really can't beat the fact that the job allows me to spend the day outdoors overlooking one of the most beautiful spots on the planet. I enjoyed chatting with both the locals and the tourists who frequented the resort, and I enjoyed the fact that my presence provided a service that, on any given day, might save lives.

I generally got along well with all the WSOs working at the resort except my new supervisor, Drake Longboard. Drake was, for lack of a better term, a jerk. I'd been working at the resort longer than he, had twice as many rescues under my belt, and ten times his instincts, yet when Mitch Hamilton, our boss, had decided to promote one of us, for some inexplicable reason he'd chosen Drake over everyone else. Cam, who had almost the same amount of experience I did, thought it was because Mitch was dating Drake's aunt, Veronica. That seemed like a lame reason to promote someone, but as hard as I've tried, I haven't been able to come up with any other reason.

"No running on the pool deck," I reminded a group of boys who looked to be nine or ten for the twentieth time in an hour.

The kids slowed down to a walk for about five steps and then took off running again. The truth of the matter was that most of the time the WSO was more of a babysitter than a lifeguard, and controlling pint-sized humans isn't what I signed up for when I decided to be a lifeguard.

"Lani to base, come in base," I said through my handheld radio.

"Hey, Lani," Cam responded. "What's up?"

"I was due for my break over an hour ago, but no one has come to relieve me."

"Drake said you already had a break."

"As usual, Drake was wrong."

"Makena came in to do breaks, but since Drake told her you'd had yours, she thought she was done for the day and left."

"Left? What do you mean, she left? I've been here for six hours and haven't so much as had the chance to pee." I knew I shouldn't take out my frustration on Cam or anyone else, but I was having a bad day and Drake's obvious attempt to mess with me was about to put me over the edge.

"Drake took off a couple of hours ago and never came back so I'm covering base, but if you give me fifteen minutes to find someone to cover the phones I'll give you a break myself."

There was no doubt about it: The situation with Drake was getting out of hand. At first Drake hadn't been left in charge all that often so it hadn't been so bad, but something was going on with Mitch, who seemed to be taking personal days more and more often. I'd asked him if things were okay, and he'd said they were, but I sensed he wasn't being completely honest with me.

With the exception of Drake, who didn't really get along with anyone, the WSOs at the resort were like a family. Joining together to save lives tended to lead to an intimacy and bonding that turns coworkers into lifelong friends.

"I'm sorry for the mix-up," Cam apologized when he came to relieve me.

"We both know it's not your fault. Drake is an idiot. I think I'm going to look for another job."

"Don't do that," Cam said. "I'm not sure what's going on exactly, but I suspect Mitch and Drake are on the outs over Drake's disappearing acts. I'm betting the situation will resolve itself."

"I hope so. I don't know how much more of the guy I can take. One of these days I'm going to unleash all my pent-up frustration and it isn't going to be pretty."

"You can't let him get to you," Cam counseled. "The more you fight him, the more he picks on you."

"I know, but he's just so..."

"Arrogant? Obnoxious? Abrasive? I get it. Drake gets on all our nerves, but if you let him goad you into doing something rash you'll be the one who winds up getting suspended."

I sighed. "I know. How long do I have?"

"Kekoa is covering the phones from the reception desk, so you're cleared for a thirty-minute break. When you get back go ahead and relieve Brody at tower two. I'll have him take over at headquarters and I'll finish the shift at the pool."

"Are you sure? I know you hate the pool almost as much as I do."

"I'm sure. You seem a little on edge today. Is everything okay?"

"Yeah," I lied. "Everything is fine."

The truth of the matter was, things weren't fine. I would never admit it to Cam or anyone else, but things were beginning to heat up between Luke and me, which left me feeling angsty and irritable. Not that anything had actually happened. As planned, I'd gone back to his place last night. We'd swum, we'd talked, we'd laughed and drunk wine, and despite the intimate setting, it was all very platonic. It wasn't what had happened that was the problem. It was what *could* have happened. The sexual tension was so thick you could have cut if with a knife. And while Luke was a perfect gentleman, I'd found myself fantasizing about how things would be if he were to take that next step into intimacy.

"Uh-oh," Kekoa greeted me as soon as I walked into the lobby. "It looks like someone woke up on the wrong side of the bed this morning."

"I'm fine. I'm just a little off today."

Kekoa just looked at me. "I'm not only your best friend, I'm your cousin. I've known you your whole life. I can tell when something's wrong."

"Tons of things are wrong." I sighed.

"Like what?"

"Drake is a jerk, I spent the morning at the family pool, and I can't decide what to do about Luke."

Kekoa got right to the heart of the matter. "How about we start with the last one? What's going on with you and Luke?"

"I think he likes me."

Kekoa looked confused. "I thought you decided you liked him too."

"I do, but I think he likes-me likes me."

"And you don't like-him like him?"

"No, I do. That's the problem."

The lobby was deserted, so Kekoa came out from around the check-in counter and walked me over to a nearby seating area. "Maybe you'd better explain exactly what's wrong," she encouraged.

I took a deep breath and let out a long sigh. Yes, I did at times have a tendency to be overly dramatic, and this was definitely one of those times, but I was feeling really funky and I needed to talk it through. "Remember when we were little girls and Leilani was dating that guy she met at the university?"

Leilani was an older cousin of ours, and Kekoa and I had idolized her when we were growing up.

"The physics major?"

"Yeah. Ben. Remember Ben?"

"Yeah, I remember Ben. What about him?"

"Do you remember how we had crushes on him and were so envious of Leilani until he broke her heart and went back to the mainland?"

Kekoa leaned forward so her elbows were resting on her knees and looked me in the eye. "I know where you're going with this. Ben broke Leilani's heart and we both vowed never to fall in love with anyone who wasn't born and raised here on the island. But that was a long time ago. We've both had casual relationships with white men."

I just looked at Kekoa.

"Oh." She paused. "You're afraid any relationship you have with Luke won't be casual." Kekoa put her hand over mine. "What are you going to do?"

"I don't know. I like Luke. I mean, I really like him. But let's face it: He's a displaced cowboy, and one of these days he's going to wake up and find living on an island claustrophobic. His entire family, his past, and probably his future, are in Texas. One of these days he's going to realize that."

I thought Kekoa might argue with me, tell me to stop worrying about something that might never happen and take the plunge with Luke. But she didn't. She knew the vow we'd made to fall in love only with men who shared both our pasts and our futures was an important one that, in the long run, really made sense. We'd actually talked about it extensively over the years. Island living was the only thing we could imagine, but it definitely wasn't for everyone.

"Have you talked to Luke about your feelings regarding falling in love with a non-Hawaiian?"

"No, not really. I guess talking about them makes them seem more real, and at this point I think I might be better off not having them at all. Sometimes I trick myself into believing I can have a relationship with Luke *and* keep it casual so that my heart isn't shattered when he eventually leaves, but he looks at me with those soulful eyes of his and I know there's no coming back from any commitment I might make to him. He has a tendency to be addictive."

"Yeah, I can see that. He really seems like a good guy and I'm sure he'll make someone a fantastic husband, but I have to agree he seems sort of displaced."

That wasn't what I wanted to hear. I wanted Kekoa to say Luke fit in perfectly and would most assuredly remain on the island forever, so I therefore had nothing to worry about.

"I know you're in a tough spot and I know it's hard right now, but…" Kekoa was suddenly interrupted by the sound of the phone ringing. "Hold that thought." She got up and walked over to the desk. "Dolphin Bay Resort." She glanced at me. "She'll be right there."

"What is it?" I asked.

"It was Brody. He needs you down at tower two to help with a rescue."

"I'm on my way."

I jumped up and ran as fast as my legs could carry me. When it comes to executing a rescue I'm all business all the time. It doesn't matter if I'm having a bad day or if I'm not feeling well or if I'm in emotional turmoil; my only thought is to save whoever needs saving in the most efficient manner possible. When I arrived at the beach I found Brody and Cam both in the water. It seemed a raft had overturned with a group of elementary-school-aged kids aboard. Cam was towing one of the kids to shore and Brody had another, but there were still several in the water. I grabbed an extra rescue can and headed into the rough sea. By the time I reached the first girl, who looked to be about ten, she was hysterical. I tucked one of the rescue cans under her arms and forced her to look at me. "How many?" I asked.

She coughed and spit out the water she'd swallowed while trying to swim to shore.

"How many?" I repeated.

"Five. There were five of us."

There were now two boys on the beach and Brody was heading toward a third boy, but I didn't see a fifth child.

"How many boys and how many girls?" I asked.

"Three boys and two girls. Me and my sister." The girl started to cry. "She's just six and she can't swim very well."

I waved for Cam to come out to pick up the girl I was talking to. "I'm going to leave you to look for your sister. Just hang on to the rescue can and don't let go, no matter what. One of the other lifeguards is coming to get you. When he gets here tell him your sister is still missing."

The girl was crying hysterically. "Don't leave me. I'm scared."

"Just hang on to the rescue can and you'll be fine. I need to find your sister, so I need you to be brave. Can you do that?"

The girl nodded. The waves were fairly big today and she was being splashed in the face, but as far as I could tell her sister was submerged and Cam would be there any minute, so I dove down, looking around frantically. Thankfully, the water was fairly clear once I got away from the waves. I gauged the current and tried to anticipate where the sister might be based on the point at which the kids had first entered the water. I prayed the entire time I swam, only surfacing to take a breath when my lungs began to burn.

It had been several minutes at least by this point. If the girl was going to live I had to find her fast. My inclination was to swim in every direction at once, but experience had taught me to focus my energy. I stopped swimming and willed my heartbeat to slow. I focused on the quiet as I stilled my mind and listened. I know this is going to sound strange and I can't really explain it, but I swear, when I'm in the middle of a rescue, if I'm able to find the place where the silence of the sea meets a focused mind, I can hear the whisper of the spirits, telling me where to find that which I seek. I let my body rest on the sea floor and concentrated my mind so my heart could listen. I could hear the surge of the water and the sound of the waves crashing in the distance. I let my mind see what my eyes couldn't. Then I slowly searched my surroundings.

Although I can hold my breath for a really long time thanks to a lifetime of free diving, I have my limits and was on the verge of needing to go up for air again when I saw something floating in the distance. Somehow my lungs found the will to hold out for a few seconds longer while I headed toward the long, dark hair that had caught my eye. I grabbed the girl and headed toward the sunlight. By the time I reached the surface my lungs were screaming for relief. I took several deep breaths before securing the girl under my arm and beginning the journey back to shore.

"She's not breathing," I informed my coworkers after dragging the girl onto the beach.

Cam and Brody began CPR as soon as we cleared the water. I fell to my knees as I took several more deep breaths. I could hear the older girl I'd rescued weeping next to me and wrapped my arms around her, holding her tight.

"Is she going to be okay?" the girl cried.

"Cam and Brody are doing everything they can. Where are your parents?"

"They're back in the room. It's just us. Please help her."

I heard sirens in the distance. Cam looked worried as he pumped the girl's chest, but I was sure the sprits wouldn't lead me to the girl only to let her die. I closed my eyes and said a silent prayer as she coughed up water and gasped for air.

# Chapter 5

You would think rescuing a child on the verge of death was a big day for me, but the truth of the matter was, executing a rescue—even one that involved a close call—was just another day at the beach. Once my shift was over I headed back to the condo to pick up Sandy and my surfboard and headed back to the beach. I knew the only thing that could really distract me from my conflicted emotions regarding Luke was a few hours on the waves, riding them in to shore as the sun set behind me.

"Oh, good, you're home." Elva stepped out onto the sidewalk that ran along the front of all six condos as I approached my front door.

"Just for a minute. I thought I'd head down the coast to see if I can find some waves."

"Have you spoken to Luke today?"

"No. I've had a busy day." I'd noticed that I had a text from him earlier; I just hadn't read it. I'd pretty much decided I needed to put some space between us until I figured out what I was going to do about him.

"Emmy Jean had lunch with Dilly and she managed to dig up some stuff on Stuart that she believes could help us with our investigation. We're all meeting at Luke's place. Janice offered to pick me up, but I told her I'd just wait and ride over with you."

So much for having some space.

"I'm pretty sure the others are already there, so we should hurry. Luke said he'd make dinner. He's a good cook, don't you think?"

"Yeah, he's the best."

"He's going to make some lucky woman a fantastic husband someday."

"I just need to change my clothes and grab Sandy. I'll meet you back out here in ten minutes."

Elva was almost bouncing with excitement. It was good to see her so happy and full of life, but I was beginning to wonder if this investigation was going to completely take over my life. Not that I minded helping the seniors, but spending every free moment with Luke wasn't going to help me to do what I knew in my heart needed to be done.

Once I was inside I decided to go ahead and check my text from Luke, which basically informed me that the seniors were heading to his house that evening and he hoped I'd be available to come along as well. I texted back, letting him know I'd be there and warning him that if he invited the women over for dinner every time they had a new clue they'd be calling him every day. He sent a return text, acknowledging that I might have a point.

I knew Cam had a date with Makena that night but wasn't sure what Kekoa's plans were, so I sent her a text, letting her know what I was doing and inviting her to join us if she was free. Then I grabbed Sandy's leash and headed out to join Elva, who was waiting for me on the community lanai.

"I wonder what Emmy Jean found out." Elva's eyes sparkled with excitement. I'd sort of expected this investigation to be hard on her, considering she'd been crushing on the victim, but she hadn't known him well, so I imagined now that the shock of his death had passed, having the opportunity to play Nancy Drew with Luke and her friends was the most exciting thing that had happened to her in a long time. "I called to try to get her to tell me what she found out, but all she would say was that she and Luke would share their news when we all arrived. You might want to watch out for that one. She seems to be going out of her way to create a sense of intimacy with your young man."

"First of all, Luke isn't my young man," I countered as I started the Jeep. "And second of all, Emmy Jean is thirty years older than Luke. I don't think I need to worry about her any more than I need to worry about Janice."

"Emmy does have those new boobs and they are pretty nice." Elva glanced at my boobs, which were nonexistent.

"Do you know whether Beth and Diane were able to speak to Susan?" I asked, effectively changing the subject.

"I did call Diane. Her daughter asked her to babysit the grandbabies, so she said she wasn't going to be able to help out with the investigation today as planned. Then I got hold of Beth, who said she'd called and left a message for Susan, who never returned her call. Beth has her class tonight, so it looks like it will just be you and me, Luke, Janice, and Emmy Jean."

"Do you think we should be worried about Susan? It's not like her to disappear the way she has. The last time anyone saw or spoke to her was at the solstice ceremony."

"I guess I am a little worried," Elva admitted. "But I'm not sure what we can do about the fact that she isn't returning our calls."

"I might mention it to Jason. Maybe he can check up on her in an official way. She's the only witness he hasn't had the chance to speak to."

The horses in the pasture nearest the drive took off running as I pulled on to Luke's private road. I wasn't a huge fan of the giant beasts, but after getting to know Lucifer, a black foal who was now three months old, I'd found I was beginning to develop a soft spot for the graceful animals. Not that I wanted to ride them or spend any time with them, but I was at the point where I could at least understand why some people might find them majestic rather than just terrifying.

When I pulled up in front of the house the first thing I noticed was that Luke was standing near the barn talking to Courtney Westlake. I'd pretty much decided Luke and I could never be anything more than friends, but the beautiful Courtney immediately made me more than a little jealous. She was everything I wasn't. I was a petite five feet, with dark skin, dark eyes, and long black hair that fell straight down my back, while Courtney was all legs and at least eight inches taller than I was, with wavy blond hair, fair skin, and blue eyes. With the exception of Lucifer, I was frightened of horses, while Courtney rode like she'd been born in the saddle. She was from Luke's home state of Texas, while I'd never been there, and she was a close friend of his family, whom I had never met. The reality was that she was as perfect for him as I was wrong, so why did my heart ache when he laughed at something she said?

Luke waved when he noticed our arrival. Courtney touched his arm intimately before she walked toward the barn and he turned and came toward us.

"We didn't mean to interrupt your conversation," I said sweetly, even though sweet wasn't the emotion I was feeling at that particular moment.

"Not a problem. We were just chatting about the mare I'm thinking about buying." Luke bent down and petted Sandy, who was thrilled to see him and not bogged down with conflicted emotions at all.

"You're buying another horse?" Elva asked.

"Perhaps. I still need to check out a few things before I commit. The others are around back, if you'd like to join them. I just need to pop into the kitchen for some more ice and I'll be around as well."

I took Elva's arm to help her navigate the brick walkway leading around the front of the house to the pool. It seemed a little odd that Luke hadn't just had us go to the pool from the house, but I supposed this route was the more direct of the two.

"I do so love this backyard," Elva commented as we rounded the corner and the pool and patio came into view.

"It really is peaceful and relaxing," I agreed. Luke had gone to a lot of effort to ensure that the landscape surrounding the pool and waterfall utilized only native plants, which gave the entire area a jungle feeling.

Elva joined Janice and Emmy Jean on the patio, where they had made themselves comfortable in the shade. I considered heading into the house to see if Luke needed any help but was afraid the seniors would see that as an attempt to have some alone time with him, which it clearly would be, so I joined them too.

Emmy Jean was wearing the most ridiculous outfit I'd ever seen. The top had absolutely no straps and appeared to be held up by the sheer will of her new boobs, and her skirt was so short it barely covered her lady parts. Now, I realize

Emmy Jean had the body to pull off such things, but the woman was old enough to be a grandmother even if she'd never wanted to ruin her body by actually having children. I looked down at my own raggedy cutoff jeans and slightly frayed tank top. I supposed there were those who might think my outfit equally inappropriate, just in a totally different way.

"Emmy Jean was just telling me that her sister, Tammy Rhea, is coming to the island later in the week," Janice informed me. "You remember Tammy Rhea, don't you, Lani?"

"Red hair, ample cleavage?"

"That'd be the one," Janice confirmed.

"Tammy Rhea has been suffering from the vapors with all the heat at home, so she's going to stay the whole summer," Emmy Jean informed me.

"That'll be nice for you," I offered.

"Tammy Rhea is my sister and I love her dearly, but she can be a bit of a handful. You know how she likes to be the center of attention. I swear, when she's around I can never get a word in edgewise. My mama, bless her soul, always said God had done blessed Tammy Rhea with the gift of gab. She can talk to anyone about anything and never miss a beat. You know, I took her to services the last time she was here and she got the pastor so distracted that he started the blessing ten minutes late."

"So you have some news about Stuart's murder?" I asked. I had a feeling Tammy Rhea wasn't the only one with the gift of gab.

"I do. I really feel it could break this case wide open."

"Luke already knows the news, so why don't you just go ahead and tell us?" Elva suggested.

"Oh, no, I couldn't do that. Big announcements require a big audience."

I didn't see how one more person was going to make for a larger audience, but I pretty much figured Emmy Jean's news was going to be nothing more than hot air so I headed over to the pool bar and helped myself to a bottle of water while I waited for Luke to get back with the ice. It did seem it was taking him an awfully long time to grab a bag and head on out. I was seriously considering heading in to track him down when he came out onto the patio with a man I didn't recognize.

"Well, hello, beautiful." The man bowed and kissed my hand. Seriously? I felt like I was in the middle of a classic black-and-white movie.

"Hello," I answered as he took my arm, escorted me back to the table where the others were sitting, and sat down next to me, all without removing his hand from my body.

"This is Clint," Luke introduced the man, who was very good-looking, but in more of a pretty boy/male model sort of way. "He's a friend from back home."

I noticed a certain tightness around Luke's mouth that I'd never seen before. If I had to guess, I'd say Luke wasn't thrilled by the visit of this particular person at this particular time.

"Luke didn't mention he had a friend in town," I commented.

"I got in just a few minutes before y'all," Clint said. "I decided to surprise the old boy, so I didn't even tell him I was coming."

"Oh, I was surprised all right," Luke replied. "These ladies and I have some private business to discuss, so perhaps you can wait for me inside."

"Luke, don't be rude," Emmy Jean scolded. "Clint has come all this way to see you; the least you could do is invite him to join us. Are you a cowboy too, sugar?"

"Clint owns a bar and restaurant near Dallas and I'm sure he's tired from his trip and would like to rest." It seemed obvious from Luke's tone of voice that his words were more than a mere suggestion.

Clint eyed me up and down in a way that made me feel like I was a bull at auction. "Luke is right, Emmy Jean. I'm sure Clint must be exhausted, and we do have that very important business to discuss," I reminded her.

"I guess I am a little tired." Clint leaned over and kissed me on the lips before he stood up. I was so shocked I almost let out a little screech, but when he did the same to both Emmy Jean and Janice I knew that must simply be his way.

Elva held out her hand when he made his way around to her and informed him that in her social circle a handshake was considered the appropriate form of greeting for a new acquaintance. Clint took her hand, pulled her close, and kissed her on the cheek.

"Oh, my." Emmy Jean held her hand to her chest as she watched Clint saunter toward the house. Even I had to admit he could fill out a pair of jeans nearly as well as Luke.

"So about this big announcement…" I attempted to get the women back on track. "What did you find out?"

Emmy Jean reluctantly turned her attention back to our group. "As you know, I had lunch with Dilly today. He wanted to go to that new place with the soup and salad bar, which seemed an odd choice because he's more of a beef-and-potatoes kind of guy. I even suggested the steak house, but he insisted on the salad bar. I mean really, have any of you ever seen the guy eat salad, or anything green for that matter?"

"So you went to lunch and then what?" I asked, trying to redirect her.

"We ordered our lunch and then I asked him about Stuart Bronson, and he told me that he was a private investigator. Can you believe that? A PI? Color me shocked. And not only was he a PI, but apparently a very high-priced one. I asked how much a high-priced PI might go for, but he declined to say."

Janice had already informed us that Stuart was a bodyguard of some sort, so his being a private investigator wasn't that much of a stretch, but Emmy Jean clearly wanted to drag out her story by repeating everything Dilly had shared with her, even if it was old news. "And did Dilly know why he was on the island and why he joined the senior group?"

"He didn't, though he did say if Stuart was on the island to find someone you could bet there was something big going on."

"Big?" Luke asked. "How big are we talking?"

Emmy Jean leaned in toward Luke before she answered. "Dilly didn't rightly know, but he did say the man wouldn't have dragged himself all the way across the ocean for a piddly little gig like a cheating husband or a runaway kid."

"How did Dilly know him?" I wondered.

"Dilly declined to say. I suspect he must have his own secret to protect. It did seem as if Dilly wasn't at all happy that Stuart had come to the island, and he did confess that when Stuart first showed up he thought he was there for *him*."

"But he wasn't?"

"Dilly said no. He said that when he confronted him about it, Stuart informed him that he was here to find someone else and Dilly could relax. He only asked Dilly to keep his cover."

I thought about the news Emmy Jean had shared. I supposed it might help, but I wouldn't exactly call it big news. On the other hand, if Stuart *was* a highly paid private investigator, the fact that he seemed to have been killed fairly easily didn't really make sense. It would seem that a PI would know how to be aware of his environment, including any personal threats, and would know how to respond.

I remembered Jason commenting that there were signs of a struggle on the body. There was no way any of the seniors present would have been able to wrestle a man who had most likely been trained in self-defense into the water. There had to have been someone else around who no one had seen, or at least no one had admitted seeing.

"Stuart told me he'd been on the island for two months. Can anyone confirm that?" I asked.

No one responded. "Is that important?" Janice asked.

"Maybe. If he had been on the island for two months and still hadn't found whoever it was he was looking for, the person must be pretty hard to find. Stuart joined the senior group for a reason; maybe his target was one of the seniors or someone related in some way to one of them. If it wasn't Dilly, who was it?"

"We could go back over the list of the people at the sunrise ceremony to see if we can figure out who Stuart was there to see," Janice suggested.

"No," Elva said. "Stuart was looking around, but it seemed as if he didn't see whoever it was he expected to find. Maybe a better use of our time would be to make a list of who was supposed to be there but didn't show up."

"What about Susan?" Luke asked. "I keep coming back to the fact that she's been missing since the ceremony. That's a pretty big coincidence."

"I agree," I chimed in. "Let's all call around to see if anyone knows anything about where she's been or how to reach her."

After dinner Elva informed me that she was getting a ride home from Janice so I was free to stay to visit with Luke for as long as I wanted. To be honest, I wasn't sure Luke even wanted me to stay. I was definitely picking up a strange vibe from him that hadn't been there the previous evening. I wanted to ask him about it, but I didn't want to let on that I was supersensitive to his every mood, so I decided to let it go.

Just as I'd made that decision, Luke said, "It's a nice evening. Care for a walk?"

"I wouldn't mind a walk. Let's take the dogs. Poor Sandy has been cooped up all day. Shredder has been taking him out when I'm at work, but he was gone today so poor Sandy missed out."

"Shredder seems like a nice guy," Luke commented as we headed down the drive toward the path that led to the bluff.

"He is."

"If Stuart had been on the island for two months it seems like he showed up at just about the same time as your new neighbor."

"Yeah, it does," I agreed. "Of course I'm sure there are a lot of other people who first arrived on the island two months ago too."

"Maybe." Luke took my hand as we left the paved trail and took to a dirt one. "How well do you know the guy?"

"Not well. I know he's a bit of a drifter who never really stays in one place for long, and other than those of us who live in the condos, he doesn't seem to have any friends, nor does he particularly seem to want any, although he's really cordial and helpful to us. I think he likes to keep things simple."

"That makes sense if he isn't planning on staying long."

"Speaking of staying long, I sort of got the vibe that you were less than thrilled to see Clint."

"Was I that obvious?"

"Probably only to me."

Luke fell in behind me as the path narrowed, leaving room for only a single person to pass at a time. "Clint is an old friend who used to be engaged to Courtney. He cheated on her and she broke up with him and moved to Oahu."

"So he's here for Courtney?" I verified.

Luke sighed. "That would be my guess. Personally, I don't think he cares about her all that much, and she's better off without him."

"He came all this way for her," I pointed out.

"I'd say he came for her because he found out she was here."

"You think he had a problem with her moving to Hawaii?"

"I think he had a problem with her moving near me."

"You used to date," I realized.

"Yeah." Luke fell in next to me as the path widened again. "In high school. Clint and I were both interested in Courtney, but she chose me, and that really hurt my relationship with him. Years later, while I was living in New York, he tried with her again, but she decided to come to New York to try again with me."

"She moved to New York to be with you?"

"For a while. When I decided to move to Hawaii she wanted nothing to do with it, so she moved back to Texas and hooked up with Clint. After they broke up she moved here, thus, I imagine, the reason for his surprise visit."

"Courtney moved to Hawaii to be with you?" I was sure my voice sounded high and squeaky.

"Not to be with me specifically, but I suppose she chose this place because she knew me and felt she needed a friend."

Okay, hold the boat. In all the time Courtney had been on the island, Luke had never mentioned that they'd ever been in a relationship or even dated. I assumed that if Courtney had moved to New York to be with Luke they must have lived together. I didn't want Luke for myself—I'd as much as decided that—but suddenly I felt like I was going to cry.

"You're probably wondering why I didn't tell you about my past relationship with Courtney before now," Luke said.

"Yeah. I guess I am. I mean, who you used to date isn't really any of my business, but it sort of seems like it might have come up in conversation."

Luke stopped walking. It was almost completely dark, but I could still see the outline of his features quite clearly. "I didn't tell you because what I had with Courtney is firmly in the past. We're friends now but nothing more, and I was afraid that if I told you about us you wouldn't give her a chance. If she's going to live here, I want you to be friends."

Friends? Was he kidding?

"So I take it Courtney isn't thrilled that Clint is here?"

"No, she isn't. She asked me to get rid of him and I told her I'd try, but he was my best friend for a lot of years and I don't feel like I can refuse to let him stay here. Having said that, I do intend to cut his visit short if I can."

I took a step back and turned toward Luke's house. "It's late; I should go."

Luke tightened his grip on my hand. "Wait. I didn't only not tell you about Courtney because I wanted you to like her. I didn't tell you about her because I want you to like *me*."

"I do like you and consider you to be a friend."

"I've been kind of hoping for more than that." Luke leaned forward and kissed me gently on the lips. It was an innocent enough kiss that only lasted for a fraction of a second, but when Luke pulled away I found myself longing for more.

# Chapter 6

## Thursday, June 30

My current schedule had me off on Sundays, Mondays, and Thursdays. I more often than not spent time with my family on Sundays and with the seniors on Mondays, but Thursdays were reserved for surfing, sleep, and Sandy. Or at least they had been until I'd gotten pulled into this investigation. Based on the text I'd received from Elva the previous evening, it looked like this particular Thursday was destined to be filled with suspects, and motives.

It wasn't that I really minded; I was having a good time with the seniors and our group activities gave me an excuse to get together with Luke without having to decide how I was going to deal with that perfectly fabulous kiss we'd shared. While we really weren't getting anywhere with the murder investigation, Jason had been able to learn that Susan had received a message right after the sunrise ceremony that her daughter was in the hospital on the mainland, so she'd left without bothering to so much as tell anyone where she was going. I wondered why she hadn't answered her phone, and she'd told Jason it was because she'd dropped it at the airport and it was still lost. Something about the whole story rang false to me, but at least I knew she was okay and didn't need to worry that something had happened to her.

The seniors weren't meeting until later that afternoon to accommodate Emmy Jean's hair and spa appointment, so I decided to take a stab at speaking to Dilly myself. Emmy Jean had said he'd revealed that Stuart was on the island to look for someone, so I had to wonder if he was some sort of a bounty hunter. True, he seemed sort of old to be in that line of work, but looks could be deceiving and perhaps he wasn't as old as he appeared.

Dilly lived on the east shore in a run-down house that happened to have a million-dollar view. He'd told the others he'd bought the property with money he'd inherited from a relative, but if Stuart was a bounty hunter and Dilly believed he was on the island to track him down, it made me wonder if there wasn't more to his inheritance than he'd let on. I didn't know Dilly well—in fact, I really didn't know him at all—but the fact that he lived right on the beach on a large piece of land hadn't escaped the notice of the other seniors, who had commented more than once about the cost of the parcel he'd purchased.

The drive along the north shore was a pleasant one and took about thirty minutes from my condo. I supposed it would have made sense to call ahead to make sure he was at home before I made the trip, but I figured if he wasn't open to talking to me the element of surprise could work to my advantage. It had been hot lately, but today there was a thick cloud cover that protected the island from the severity of the summer sun. I'd taken the top off my Jeep before strapping Sandy in to the passenger seat, allowing the wind to blow through my hair as I sang along to the oldies I enjoyed playing. The only downside of a cloudy day was that the ocean's aqua blue water took on a muddy gray tint, though during the summer months I found I'd trade a cooling trend for color on almost any day.

I turned off the main road and on to the private drive as soon as I arrived at the address I'd been given by Emmy Jean. It looked as if Dilly's car was there, which I took as a good sign. I unbuckled Sandy and made my way to the front door, which looked as if it hadn't been used for some time. Dilly's car had been pulled around to the side of the house, so my guess was that he used the back door as a means of entry, as did a lot of folks on the island. I decided to try the front door first, though; going around to the back seemed sort of invasive. When Dilly didn't answer I headed around to the back, where I found him fishing off the pier.

"What are you doing here?" Dilly greeted me in a less-than-friendly manner.

"I had a few questions and hoped you'd have a few minutes to chat."

"Well, I don't, so you best get on now."

I ignored him and launched into my rehearsed speech. "I understand you knew Stuart Bronson prior to his arrival on the island."

"I told you, I ain't answering no questions."

I took a deep breath and tried to quell my irritation. "I'm trying to track down a killer."

"And I'm trying to catch my dinner. Now you get on outta here before I have to have you arrested for trespassing."

"Look, if you're afraid I'm going to interfere in your personal life you don't need to worry. That isn't why I'm here. I just want to try to figure out who might have killed Stuart, and I figured if you knew him, you might be able to point me in a direction."

Dilly reeled in his line and turned as if to return to the house.

"If you won't talk to me I'll have no choice but to have my cop brothers research you and your connection to Mr. Bronson," I threatened. "They might not be as apt to turn a blind eye to whatever secrets you seem so intent on keeping as I am."

Dilly stopped walking. He turned around and looked at me. "I knew I shouldn't have gotten involved with that dangnab senior group. Too many people thinking they have a right to know all about me. It's not right. I keep to myself and don't bother no one."

"I have a theory," I continued, ignoring his outburst. "My theory is that Stuart Bronson was some sort of bounty hunter, and when he came to the senior group you recognized him because you're hiding out here and there's a bounty on your head. Am I close?"

"Might be, but then again, you might not. Now if you will excuse me, I think I'm going to head inside."

Well, that had been a waste of time. Dilly hadn't actually told me anything. I did notice, though, that when I'd referred to Stuart as a bounty hunter Dilly had looked almost relieved. I found it odd that he would be relieved by an accusation that he was wanted by the law, but unless I'd totally misread things, there was something much worse he didn't want me finding out.

I still had a couple of hours before I was supposed to meet up with Elva and take her to Luke's for our Nancy Drew meeting, so I grabbed my surfboard and headed to the beach. There was nothing that helped to clear my mind better than riding the giant waves, although you really couldn't refer to the waves as giant today. I left Sandy playing on the beach while I paddled out into the water toward the other surfers waiting to catch a wave. As I approached the line, I noticed there was a small pod of dolphins swimming among the men and women who'd gathered.

Although seeing dolphins while surfing in Hawaii is common, I can still remember the first time I'd surfed with the beautiful creatures. I must have been around four years old and my dad had taken me to a spot he knew where dolphins were apt to be seen. It was early in the morning and my brothers were all in school, so it was just the two of us. We swam out beyond the break and my dad schooled me to sit quietly and wait for them to come to us. I'd seen dolphins from a distance many times, but that first time, as they swam up to greet me, I knew I would never leave the island I loved.

I realize not everyone feels the same way about the island that I do. A lot of the kids I grew up with had moved to the mainland the minute they'd graduated high school. Personally, I don't understand why anyone would want to move away from everything and everyone familiar to them, but I supposed those kids were a lot like Luke in that they wanted to experience a larger slice of the world.

Emmy Jean's sister, Tammy Rhea, had decided to come to the meeting to get a look at the cowboy everyone had been talking about. With the exception of her red hair, she was a lot like Emmy Jean in terms of the way she dressed and presented her assets. I couldn't decide who actually talked more, but I had a feeling very little sleuthing was going to be accomplished in the presence of the southern sisters.

"Tammy Rhea wanted to have her roots colored before the dance at the senior center on Saturday, but the girls at the Cut and Curl had no idea how to duplicate her specific shade of red, so we had to drive all the way down to Waikiki and go to one of those expensive salons that can match pretty much any color you can imagine," Emmy Jean explained when the sisters arrived later than the others. "And once we made the trip all the way down there we decided to splurge on mani/pedis." Emmy Jean waved her red nails in front of her face for effect. "I wanted something classy, but Tammy Rhea decided to color her toes bright purple. Tammy Rhea, show the girls your toes."

Tammy Rhea slipped off her shoe and hoisted her leg into the air so we could all see her bright purple toes.

"That's real pretty, Emmy Jean, but we're here to talk about the investigation," Janice reminded her.

"Not until the cowboy gets back with the sweet tea," Tammy Rhea insisted. "It wouldn't be polite to start until everyone was present."

"I'll go check on Luke and the tea," I offered. I love my time with the seniors and I look forward to spending time with them, but thoughts of the situation with Luke had left me feeling unsettled, and if I had to listen to the sisters yapping for much longer I was going to blow my brains out.

I walked into the kitchen hoping for a few minutes of quiet only to find Luke chatting with Courtney. I almost turned around and walked right back out, but Luke saw me and waved me forward. "The ladies are asking about the tea," I said.

"It's right here." Luke nodded toward a frosty pitcher.

"I don't suppose you have regular tea?" I asked. "If not, water is fine."

"Not a fan of the sweet stuff?"

"Not even a little bit."

"We'll figure this out after the women leave," Luke said to Courtney before picking up the pitcher and turning toward the patio.

"Thanks, Luke." Courtney stood on tiptoe and kissed him on the cheek before she left.

"Problem?" I asked as casually as I could manage as I followed him out.

"Not really. Clint has been bugging her, and she asked me to try to get him to back off. I'll talk to him later."

"After we all leave?"

"After the others leave. I was sort of hoping you'd stay."

I didn't answer, mainly because I had no idea what that answer would be. I knew I should stay away from Luke, and when I wasn't with him it seemed doable, but when he smiled at me with his sexy grin or looked at me with his deep blue eyes, I found myself melting inside. Besides, the territorial part of my mind wasn't a fan of leaving Luke in the hands of the gorgeous Courtney.

Once the tea had been served, Luke asked the women if they had anything to share. When Emmy Jean went off on her trip to the south shore and the spa treatments she and Tammy Rhea had received, Luke quickly clarified that what he was really asking was what they had to share pertaining to the murder investigation they were determined to be involved in.

"As you all know, I missed the previous meeting because I was at my class," Beth began. "But as it turned out, I picked up what I feel is a significant clue while I was there."

"Do tell." Emmy Jean clapped her diamond-ringed hands together in a gesture of excitement.

"It seems one of my classmates witnessed a man fitting Stuart's description coming and going from a house on the street where she lives several times during the past several weeks."

"And where does your friend live?" I asked.

"Wahiawa. She said the only reason she even noticed him was because he was wearing a business suit and it's been hotter than Hades."

I frowned. It did seem odd that Stuart had worn a suit around town. If he really were some sort of highly paid investigator or bounty hunter or the like, you would think he'd be a master at blending in, yet wearing a full suit in Hawaii was anything but.

"Did your classmate have a feeling for what he might have been doing or who he might have been doing it with?" I asked.

"No, but she gave me an address." Beth handed me a piece of paper.

I looked at Luke. "Are you up for a drive?"

"I'm in." Luke looked around at the others. "Does anyone have anything else?"

"I have something." Emmy Jean raised her hand as if she were in a classroom.

"Yes, Emmy Jean?" Luke gifted her with a smile that could only be referred to as charming.

"I called my cousin Annabelle Lee, who's married to her high school sweetheart, Billy Don John, and asked her if she could have him look into Stuart's past. Billy Don John works for the local sheriff in the little town where Tammy Rhea and I grew up. He's not a deputy or anything, but he does handle the records and is in charge of doing background searches and whatnot. Anyway, I knew it was a long shot because I didn't have a lot of information on Stuart Bronson other than his name and general description, but apparently Billy Don John is really gifted at his job, and he found three men with the name Stuart Bronson who had prior records and fit the age and height of our man."

"And...?" I asked.

"And he sent me photos."

Emmy Jean passed a large envelope across the table. I opened it and pulled out three photos. "This is him." I held up the second photo from the bottom. "Did Billy Don John have any other information on him?"

"Turn the photo over. What he had is on the back."

It wasn't a lot. It simply said that Stuart Bronson was born and raised in Washington, D.C., and that he had been arrested for stalking a congressman but was never convicted. Okay, that was weird. It sounded like a piece of news I might want to share with Jason.

"Did I help?" Emmy Jean cooed.

"You helped." Luke gave her another of his million-dollar smiles, causing Emmy Jean to flush from the roots of her bleached-blond hair down to the tips of her red-painted toes.

# Chapter 7

After the women left I called Jason and shared with him the information Emmy Jean had given us. As usual, he already knew all about Stuart Bronson, including the fact that his criminal as well as his military records had been sealed. I could tell he wasn't going to give me much more than that, so I chatted about his wife Alana and his kids for a few minutes and then got off the phone.

I wasn't sure taking a drive to Wahiawa to check out the address Beth had given us was worth the effort, but I still wasn't ready to leave Luke alone with Courtney, whose car I saw was still in the drive, even though I likewise wasn't sure I was ready to stay for strictly social reasons.

Janice offered to take Elva home and Sandy seemed thrilled to be left with Luke's dogs, Duke and Dallas, so it was just Luke and me who set out on the drive into the center of the island.

"I love Elva and I love her friends, but after listening to Emmy Jean and Tammy Rhea talking nonstop for two hours I'm happy for the quiet," I commented.

"My sisters can talk up a southern storm, but I get what you're saying. Still, I have to admit the sisters from the south are beginning to make me homesick. It's been a while since I've heard a good, drawn-out y'all."

"Have you been home to visit since moving here?" I wondered.

"Not so far. First I was dealing with the remodel on the house and then my family started visiting me in droves, so there didn't seem to be a reason to make the trip. I suppose I might think about going over the holidays this year."

It made me sad to think of Luke not being here then.

"I noticed Courtney doesn't seem to have much of an accent at all, even though I remember you saying she was brought up near where you lived."

"Courtney had a very cultured upbringing in which slurring and slang were frowned upon. My own mother wasn't a fan of southern dialect, which is why I don't have much of an accent either. When I moved to New York I lost what little I had."

"Clint, on the other hand, sounds exactly the way I'd picture a cowboy sounding, although he doesn't look much like a cowboy."

"Clint can be whoever he needs to be to get what he wants at any given time."

"It sounds like you still aren't getting along."

"We're tolerating each other for the time being. At some point I'm going to have to keep my promise to Courtney and get rid of him."

"It seems to me Courtney's relationship with Clint is her problem, not yours. She's a big girl; I'd let her handle it herself. If she doesn't want to confront Cliff she can stay away from your place until he leaves."

Luke smiled and put his hand over mine on the seat between us. "That's one of the things I like best about you. You're fiercely independent and willing to fight your own battles."

"I thought that's what you found most frustrating about me."

Luke squeezed my hand. "It was. At first. But I'm learning to adapt. Lani Pope, you're a special kind of woman and I'm a better man for having known you."

I tried to suppress the grin that was threatening to take over my entire face. The last thing I wanted was for Luke to know how much his words meant to me. "Take a left at this next intersection," I instructed.

Luke did so and continued to follow my instructions regarding three more turns. Eventually, we arrived at the street we were looking for. We parked in front of the address Beth had given us. The house looked to be empty, which I guess made it the perfect location for Stuart to do whatever it was he was doing.

"What now?" Luke asked.

"I'm not sure." I looked around. "I'd say we should see if we can get inside, but I don't want anyone to think we're breaking in and call the cops."

"There's a fence around the backyard. We can sneak into the back to see if we can get inside that way. It might be best to go up and knock on the door first, though, just in case the house isn't deserted."

"I'll go knock on the door," I offered. "If someone answers I'll make up some lame story about having the wrong house, and if no one answers we'll sneak around to the back."

"Maybe I should be the one to knock on the door," Luke suggested.

I looked at his tight jeans and cowboy boots. "I blend in and you stick out like a cowboy in Hawaii. I'll knock on the door, but you can watch my back."

Luke grinned.

"My back, not my butt."

I hopped out of the truck and went up the front walk. I knocked on the door and waited for approximately ten seconds. Then I knocked again and looked in the window. The place looked to be empty. I waved for Luke to join me and then went around to the side of the house, searching for a way to access the back. The gate was locked, but I was well skilled in scaling fences, so I hopped over and got into the house through a rear window that happened to be open. Once I was inside I hurried to the front and opened the door for Luke just as he arrived there.

The house looked like any other, the furniture ordinary and fairly drab, leading me to believe it might have been rented as a furnished unit. I didn't see any personal mementos on the tabletops or any pictures on the walls. The kitchen as well as the entry bath were spotless and appeared to be unused. The cupboards and refrigerator were empty, although I did find a cup in one of the trash cans, along with a wadded-up gum wrapper with a telephone number written on it. I used my cell to call the number, which was answered by an operator at a local military base. Interesting.

I wandered down the hall and into a bedroom. The closet was as empty as the medicine cabinet in the bathroom and the cabinets in the kitchen. Whatever Stuart had been doing in the house, he hadn't been living here. I looked at the discarded cup. It was a coffee cup from a gas station, probably the one down the street. I supposed it wouldn't hurt to follow up to see if Stuart had bought coffee while in the neighborhood.

"There's not a lot here," Luke said when he joined me.

"No." I sighed. "There isn't."

I couldn't help being disappointed. I'd hoped that by finding a house Stuart had been known to visit we would discover clues more valuable than an empty coffee cup and a gum wrapper. Of course, if he really was some sort of a bounty hunter he'd probably be pretty good at covering his tracks.

I knew it was a long shot, but I figured asking the clerk at the gas station if he'd seen Stuart wouldn't be a total waste of time. I still had the photo Emmy Jean had provided, so if Stuart *had* bought the coffee at that establishment someone might remember him. I took a few random photos of the house and tabletops with my cell for the heck of it before Luke and I headed back to the car. You never knew when you'd have occasion to want to remember something you'd seen in the past. One of the things I'd learned while studying to be the best detective Hawaii had ever seen was that just because you didn't see anything that seemed important to your case, that didn't mean there wasn't anything there.

The drive to the gas station took only a few minutes. Once again I deemed it would be important for me to go in alone. Luke was a great guy, but he really did stick out like a sore thumb.

"Aloha," the clerk, who looked to be in his late teens, greeted me with a smile.

"Aloha," I answered. "I was wondering if you could help me out."

The kid just grinned at me.

"I'm looking for a friend who's been staying in the area and I was wondering if you'd seen him." I showed the boy the photo.

"Yeah, I've seen him. He was in a couple of times, although I haven't seen him for more than a week. Guess he might have moved on. Seemed like a tourist to me."

"And when he was here he bought coffee?"

"No. The haole he met bought coffee. The guy you're looking for never bought a thing. Not even gas. Not sure why they thought this was a good place for a meeting."

"They came in separately?"

"Yeah. The younger guy would get here about ten minutes before the one in the suit. The younger guy would buy a cup of coffee and then he'd sit on the bench out front and wait. As soon as the other one showed up, they'd chat and then they'd both leave in the younger guy's car."

"And the older man's car?"

"He left it in the lot across the street."

"Can you describe the younger guy?"

"White guy but with a decent tan. Long hair, light. Looked like he could live here or maybe some other beach location. We chatted a few times about surfing and it was obvious he knew his stuff."

I hated to even think it, but the first person I thought of was Shredder, who seemed like a man with both a past and a secret, although I didn't like the idea that he was in any way involved in a murder.

"Anything else you can remember about the guy the man in the suit met?" I asked. "Even a small detail. A tattoo, an unusual piece of jewelry, maybe an accent or a physical identifier like crooked teeth, eye color, dimples?"

Okay, I was grasping at straws, but I really needed this guy to eliminate Shredder for my own peace of mind.

"Didn't notice dimples or even eye color. He had dark glasses on. Teeth were straight and white. He did have a small tattoo on his underarm. I don't know what it was, but I did wonder about the placement."

"His underarm?"

The kid lifted his arm and pointed to his armpit.

I frowned. That did seem like an odd placement. "How did you manage to even see the tattoo?"

"I was stocking shelves when he came in one day. I started to climb down from the footstool and bumped into the top shelf with my shoulder. It started to fall and the guy reached up to steady it. That's when I noticed the tattoo. I'm sure it was a word, or maybe a symbol. It was small and I only got a quick look, so I can't say for sure."

Okay, now all I had to do was get Shredder to raise his arms into the air to see if he had a tattoo. Piece of cake. I thanked the clerk for his time and the info and returned to Luke and the truck. I explained what the clerk had told me, which hadn't really meant much other than to create a suspicion in my mind regarding Shredder.

"So what now?" I asked. "I can take the cup to Jason so he can test it for fingerprints or DNA or whatever, although if I do that he's going to wonder where I got it, and that's going to open up a whole new can of worms."

"Maybe we should have dinner and discuss it," Luke suggested.

"Are you hungry? There's a pretty good pizza place down the road."

"I have something different in mind if you're up for a drive."

I shrugged. "Yeah, I'm good with it. What are you thinking?"

Luke smiled. "It's a surprise."

I'd lived on the island all my life, so I doubted Luke could surprise me. Still, the last time we'd gone sleuthing he'd taken me to a cowboy restaurant that was nowhere on my radar.

"I noticed Courtney's car was still at your place when we left. Do you think she's waiting for you to come back to finish your conversation?"

"I texted her to say I was out with you so she should just lay low for a day or two until I got the chance to speak to Clint."

"I bet she loved that," I mumbled under my breath.

"Loved what?"

"The fact that you put her request on hold because you were out with me. I'm not trying to butt into your personal life, but why else would she follow you here unless she was looking to rekindle your romantic relationship?"

"We're just friends."

"Are you sure? She does have a pattern of following you wherever you go, and it sounds like she had more than friendship on her mind in the past."

I saw Luke frown before he once again assured me that wasn't the case this time around and they really were just friends. I couldn't say for sure, but I thought there was a chance I'd put at least a little doubt in his mind.

The restaurant he took me to on the west shore was really more of a shack with a few tables on the beach. I was pretty sure it was a private residence, much like Dilly's, where the occupant had a ten-dollar house built on a million-dollar lot. The restaurant owner was named Biff and the entire place seemed to consist of no more than the tables set out on the beach overlooking a gorgeous sea.

I will say that when Luke first pulled up I wasn't impressed. We were shown to a table for two on which a chilled bottle of champagne already waited. I figured Luke must have called ahead. The menu consisted of whatever fish Biff had caught that day, along with island fruit and rice. The starter was a shrimp salad with locally grown greens, followed by the fish of the day, which was served with rice and pineapple salsa that was to die for. There was a delicious dipping sauce of unknown origin, accompanied by grilled veggies that must have been purchased that morning from the farmers market.

"What is in this sauce?" I asked.

"No one other than Biff knows. I think it's what keeps people coming back. It's addictive."

I took another bite. "It really is. And even though I'm pretty sure Biff's restaurant probably isn't legal, I agree the food is awesome. I guess as long as there aren't any complaints from his neighbors he won't get shut down."

"He feeds his neighbors a free meal once a week. Keeps them happy, and happy neighbors are less likely to narc you out."

Luke was an enigma. He came up with the most unique and interesting dates—if you could even consider this a date, which clearly it wasn't.

"I ran into one of your brothers the other day," he said.

"Really? Which one?" I had five brothers—John, Jason, Jimmy, Justin, and Jeff—or, as my mom referred to them, the J team.

"Jimmy. I was with my sister and her family on Kauai and I saw a cop in a coffee shop. He looks a lot like you, so I took a chance and asked if he was related to you, and he said he was your middle brother."

"Yeah, he's number three out of five. Was he curious how a cowboy like you would know a native Hawaiian like me?"

"Nope; he said he'd heard all about me from Jason and Jeff and was really happy to finally meet the man who'd managed to tame his sister. Have I managed to tame you?"

"Not by a long shot, and when I next see my brothers I'll make sure they know just how untamed I am."

Luke just laughed.

"It's really a pain having so many brothers. They treat me like a kid."

"Well, I'm going on record to say I don't in any way see you as a kid. As far as I can tell, you're at least as smart, intuitive, and capable as anyone I've ever met. I sort of get the big brother thing, though. I'm the youngest, so I don't have any little sisters, but I've seen my older brothers watching over my sisters, and I have to say there are times I can identify with the need to protect the women in your life."

My lips tightened as I prepared my reply, but Luke must have notice because he quickly added, "It's the cowboy code to watch over our women. We agreed to disagree on this one."

"You're right, we did. Just don't try any of that protective stuff with me."

Luke crossed his hand over his chest.

"So about the case..." I began, deciding to change the subject to something a bit more neutral and less controversial. "Any idea what to do next?"

"Not really. We don't have a lot of leads and the ones we do have don't seem to be going anywhere."

"We've learned a few things today that may prove to be relevant, although I'm not sure how," I informed him.

Luke leaned forward and looked directly at me. I loved the way he seemed to pay complete attention to what I had to say. "Okay, what do you have?"

"When I called my brother to tell him about the information Emmy Jean had dug up he told me he already knew all that but was having a hard time expanding on it because Stuart's criminal and military records were sealed."

"So he was in the military," Luke realized.

"Exactly. And I've been thinking about that. Initially, Emmy Jean told us that Dilly mentioned Stuart was on the island to retrieve something. And Dilly initially said he was nervous seeing Stuart because he knew he was on the island to find someone, though he assured Dilly he was here to find someone else, so he could relax. Stuart only asked that Dilly keep his cover. When I dropped in on Dilly today I postulated that Stuart was some sort of a bounty hunter and Dilly recognized him as such and was nervous he was here for him because he was a fugitive from the law. Dilly didn't confirm or deny it, but he did seem relieved when I made the assumption that he was running from the law."

"Which is an odd reaction, especially when you have five brothers who are cops."

"It did make me wonder what could be worse than being a fugitive from the law, but I've been noodling on the comment Jason made about the military, and it occurred to me that perhaps Stuart worked for the government or a government agency like the CIA or perhaps the military. I found a gum wrapper in the trash at the house that turned out to have the number of a nearby military base."

"I guess that fits with the fact that Stuart's records are sealed. Any idea how we can find out for sure?"

"Dilly. I couldn't get him to talk, but he clearly knows more than he's letting on. Emmy Jean got him to talk by getting him drunk. I think maybe we should try a similar tactic again."

"You think if you show up with a bottle of tequila he'll let his guard down and talk to you?"

"No, but he might talk to Emmy Jean again. I have a plan."

My idea involved Emmy Jean calling Dilly and asking him to meet her and Tammy Rhea at a bar not far from where he lived. It was my opinion that Dilly would jump at the chance to have drinks with two beautiful women. The bar I selected had private booths and I knew that, although you couldn't see the person in the booth behind you, if you listened carefully you could hear the conversation being held there. I wanted Emmy Jean to steer Dilly to the booth I'd reserved for just that purpose.

Luke and I finished our meal and headed back to the north shore while Emmy Jean called Dilly and made the arrangements. She got back to me to confirm that he was going to meet them at the bar at nine. That would give Luke and me time to get back around the island and get into position. While Luke drove, I filled Emmy Jean in on the information we were seeking. I also arranged to text comments and additional questions to the women throughout their conversation.

Emmy Jean and Tammy Rhea were already there when Luke and I arrived. Luckily, they had managed to save two booths that were situated back to back and would work perfectly. I made sure both women had turned off their cell phone ringers so Dilly wouldn't be aware they were receiving texts. I ordered and paid for a bottle of the whiskey Emmy Jean swore was Dilly's favorite and Luke and I got into position.

The sisters sat discussing the latest celebrity gossip while they waited for Dilly. I just hoped he would bother to show up after all the effort we'd gone to. Happily, he did and was more than happy to help the women take care of the bottle of whiskey they'd ordered.

It was hard to sit patiently and wait for the alcohol to begin to take effect. Emmy Jean told Dilly all about their day at the spa while he downed his first few shots and the story was even more boring the second time around. Luke hadn't heard it in his house because he'd been in the kitchen with Courtney, and based on the smile on his face, he was enjoying the tale the two women were almost acting out.

The sisters and I had rehearsed several opening statements that I'd hoped would steer the conversation in the direction we hoped.

"So where are you from, sugar?" Tammy Rhea asked. "I swear I can detect just a hint of a southern drawl in your voice."

"Kentucky originally, but I haven't lived there since before I went into the military."

"If there's one thing I love it's a man in the military," Tammy Rhea drawled. "Do you still have your uniform?"

"No. I got rid of that a long time ago."

"Too bad. There's nothing quite like a man in uniform to get my engine running."

"Oh, I think I could manage to get your engine running just fine even without the uniform."

"Do you have any tats?" Tammy Rhea asked. "I love a man with tats."

"Used to have a couple of them, but I had them removed. I can show you the scars if you'd like."

He must have done just that because we heard Tammy Rhea giggle.

"Were you in Afghanistan?" Emmy Jean asked.

"Vietnam."

"And you didn't stay in the military after Nam?"

"No, I got out. Would you like another drink?"

"I would," Emmy Jean said. "I can't believe we downed that whole bottle. I'm having the best time."

"I think I'd better take a break or you're going to have to carry me out of here." Tammy Rhea giggled again.

I hoped both women had remembered to dump their whiskey into the glass they'd hidden between them when Dilly wasn't looking so they wouldn't really get drunk.

"Now don't you worry your pretty little head about having too much to drink," Dilly insisted. "When I was in the army I used to have a reputation for being able to outdrink everyone else, which also meant I ended up being the one who made sure everyone got home safe. They used to call me Taxi Tom."

"Taxi Tom? I thought your name was Dilly." Tammy Rhea managed to pull off the perfect blend of confused fascination."

"Is now. Back then my name was Tom."

"I like the name Tom," Tammy Rhea commented. "It's such a strong name. I bet you were a good soldier."

Dilly laughed. "There are those who would disagree with you about that."

It seemed Dilly was beginning to slur his words just a bit. It was time to focus the conversation, so I texted Emmy Jean to tell her to ask about Stuart.

"You know," Emmy Jean began, "Stuart, that man who died, was in the military. I think he said he was in the army. Did you boys belong to the same unit? It seemed like you knew each other."

"We were both in the army, but we weren't in the same unit. I never even met the guy until the day he showed up at the senior center."

"Really?" Emmy Jean poured on the surprise. "I could swear you recognized the man."

"Oh, I recognized him all right. I'd just never met him. Either of you girls interested in moving this party back to my place?"

"Before we finish the bottle?" Tammy Rhea sounded scandalized.

Unfortunately, Dilly had decided to speed things up by downing the remainder of the bottle and passed out a short time later. We piled him into Luke's truck and drove him home, and I took a photo of him on the sofa where we'd left him. I had a feeling Dilly and Stuart's pasts and the point at which they intersected would end up being an important clue in the future.

# Chapter 8

## Friday, July 1

On Friday morning I forwarded Jason the photo I'd taken of Dilly, along with the information that he'd fought in Vietnam, where his name had been Tom. We'd also learned that he'd originally come from Kentucky, and that it seemed like he was on the run for some reason not only because he'd changed his name but because he'd also had tattoos removed. I'd managed to slip the glass from which Dilly had been drinking into my backpack and arranged for someone to come by the resort during my shift to pick it up to take to the police station.

"Did you see the new schedule Mitch posted?" I asked Cam when he showed up to give me my first break.

"Yeah, I saw it."

"What is he thinking? We've had the same shifts for months, with the same days off, and now, out of nowhere, he changes everything around. It makes no sense."

"I know the schedule looks as if it came from Mitch—and because he's the one who posts the schedules, there's really no reason to question it—but I came in early and saw Drake making the changes."

"Figures. Can he do that?"

"I suppose so, unless Mitch has a problem with it. He's Mitch's assistant. For all we know, Mitch authorized the changes, although I haven't seen him all day, so I'm not sure if he's even aware a new schedule has been posted."

I jumped down off my tower. "Well, I'm not going to stand by and let Drake mess up my plans without a very good reason. I'll call Mitch at home if I have to."

"I'd be careful if I were you. For some reason Mitch is letting Drake do pretty much whatever he wants. I thought he might be planning to can the guy, but so far he hasn't done a thing about all the problems he's causing and the shifts he's missing."

"I'll be careful. Are we still hitting the beach tonight?"

"That's the plan. Of course, I used to have tomorrow off and now I have to work, so it might be an earlier night than I thought."

"I was supposed to work tomorrow, but now I have it off and have to work on

Sunday, which will interfere with my plans with my family. Do you want to trade?"

"I would, but Makena had her schedule switched around as well and now we both have Sunday off. Sorry."

"That's okay." I sighed. "I don't want to mess up your date. I'll be back in twenty."

I jogged off toward the lobby in the hope that Kekoa wouldn't be busy and I could vent about how badly I wanted to haul off and slug Drake. One of these days my temper was going to get the better of me and I was going to do just that. I could honestly say I didn't remember how the rivalry between Drake and me even started. I did know, though, that there were several things about both his personality and his looks that grated on my nerves, so chances were it somehow got back to the egotist that I'd referred to him as a shaggy dog who spent most of each day chasing his own tail.

When I entered the lobby I found my brother Jason chatting with Kekoa. I was surprised; this was the first time Jason had ever visited the Dolphin Bay Resort except in an official capacity, such as when that developer had been found dead on the beach a few months earlier.

"What are you doing here?" I asked.

"I was just on my way out to find you and stopped to say hi to Kekoa. Do you have a minute?"

"I need to be back in fifteen."

"That's enough time. Let's use a table in one of the empty conference rooms. It's best we aren't overheard."

Okay, this conversation definitely had the possibility of going one way or another. Given the fact that Jason wanted privacy, I figured either I'd done something to get myself into trouble again or my brother was actually interested in discussing the case with me.

"Are you here for the glass?" I asked as we sat down. "I have it in my locker."

"No, we don't need the glass. I managed to track down Dilly's real identity through the other information you gave me. It seems his name is actually Thomas Carter, and he *is* from Kentucky. He was drafted when he was eighteen and spent two years overseas. He worked in requisitions, which allowed him to very cleverly create a quite profitable side business."

"A side business?"

"He skimmed supplies off the top from every delivery and recorded them as being damaged in some way. Then he sold them on the black market."

"He stole supplies from our men for profit?"

Jason nodded. "He was caught eventually and brought up on charges. He'd managed to amass quite a bit of money and was looking at a pretty good amount of jail time. Somehow he managed to escape while being transported and hadn't been seen since."

"Until now."

"Until now. One of my men picked him up this morning. He was turned over to the military shortly after."

"You turned him over to the military? Why? He was our best shot at figuring out what happened to Stuart."

"I didn't really have a choice."

"Did he tell you anything before custody was transferred?"

"Not officially, but he did mention to the officer who picked him up that he was done with whiskey. He kept going on and on about how he got sloppy when he figured he was safe. I guess Stuart had been looking for him for a very long time and when Stuart made it clear he was a small fish he wasn't here for, he let down his guard."

I frowned. Stuart had been looking for Dilly for a very long time?

"That got me thinking." Jason expressed what I'd begun to think. "It seems to make sense that Stuart worked for the military, tracking down fugitives. I asked the military police who picked Carter up if that was true, but all they would say was that he didn't currently work for the military in any capacity."

"Currently? So maybe in the past?"

"That would be my guess. I'm going to explore this angle to the extent I'm able, given the fact that the man's records are sealed. I thought I'd fill you in just in case you heard something that might help us."

"Yeah, I'll let you know."

"And leave the follow-up to me. If you get a clue call me to let me handle it."

"I will."

Jason looked doubtful.

"I swear."

"Okay, good. I wouldn't want you getting hurt. Mom would kill me if she suspected I was letting you help me."

"Don't worry; I'll be careful and she'll never know. And Jason...thanks."

Jason tweaked me on the nose like he'd done when I was a kid and walked away. I had no doubt all my brothers looked at me as some kind of a kid who needed to be coddled and looked out for, so it meant a lot to me that Jason was keeping me in the loop, at least to a minor degree.

Of all my brothers, Jason probably had been the most adamant that I wasn't cut out to be a cop. My oldest brother, John, who's a detective for the Maui PD, could be protective as well, but overall he had a much more laid back personality than Jason, who was all serious, all the time. My middle brother, Jimmy, who works for the Kauai PD, really embraced his middle-child role by acting as peacemaker and all-around good guy more often than not. I loved all my brothers and wanted all of them to be proud of me, but I find it's Jason I most want to impress.

After Jason left I returned to my tower just as Cam came on the radio to track me down. We'd had a shark bite and he needed help clearing the water.

"How bad is it?" I asked as I grabbed my rescue can.

"Male victim, midtwenties, bite to right shoulder while surfing. It looks bad but not fatal. The paramedics are on the way; right now we just need to get the water cleared."

I ran toward the waterline as hundreds of swimmers, surfers, and tubers ran toward shore in a mass panic. I could hear Cam instructing people to exit the water in a calm and efficient manner as I scanned the area for the shark, which was believed to still be in the area. I didn't see it, but I did see swimmers being knocked to the ground as hordes of others exited the water en masse. There were still hundreds of people in the water but only one of me, so I couldn't respond to every man, woman, and child who'd been knocked down. What I could do was keep an eye out for anyone who'd fallen but didn't appear to be getting back up.

Years of watching the water had allowed me to develop a sense for who was actually in trouble and who would be able to make it on their own. Generally, I had a sense of who to watch and who to scan past. As soon as I saw a group of teenage surfers surging toward shore, I knew there was going to be trouble. Unfortunately, I was right, and I cringed as one of the surfers ran into a young boy on a raft, dumping him into the water.

I ran into the water and began swimming toward the boy while everyone else headed out of the water all around me. Talk about swimming upstream. It wouldn't take much for me to lose sight of the location where the boy had gone down in all the chaos, but I forced myself to maintain my focus and my calm. By the time I reached the spot where I'd seen the boy submerge, the area had cleared. I dove down and, luckily, found him after only a brief search. He had a gash on his head that I assumed he'd received when he was trampled.

I grabbed him and swam to the surface. When we cleared the water I tucked my rescue can under his head before beginning mouth-to-mouth. Fortunately, he hadn't been under long and began to breathe almost immediately. Of course, the second he came to he began to panic, and I knew I had only seconds to get the situation under control.

"My name is Lani. What's yours?" I asked as I tucked the rescue can under the boy's arms so he could hang, allowing him to float on the surface of the water.

"Casey."

"Okay, Casey. You and I are going to swim to shore together, but I need you to calm down and let me do the swimming. Can you do that?"

"There's a shark."

"I know, which is why we need to get out of the water. It will go faster if you're perfectly calm. The rescue can will help you to float, so you don't need to worry about going under again."

The boy pointed to something over my shoulder. "What about the shark?"

I turned around. Damn. The shark was less that ten yards behind me. I turned and faced the boy, wrapping my arms around him with the rescue can between us. "Okay, plan B," I said in the calmest voice I could manage. "We're going to float right here and stay perfectly still. Don't kick your legs or splash the water in any way."

"Shouldn't we try to swim away?"

"No. Sharks are attracted to movement, especially movement that creates surface splashing. The reality is, there's no way we can outswim that shark, so we're just going to wait here quietly until he goes away. I'm going to turn us around slowly so I can see the shark. I need you to be as still as possible and let me do the work."

"Okay."

I slowly turned us around, being careful not to splash the surface of the water or make any big movements. The shark was continuing to swim in our vicinity, but right then he didn't seem to be paying any attention to us. I could feel my heart beating in my chest as I watched the large mammal, trying to predict his next move.

"Is he gone?" the boy whispered in my ear.

"No," I whispered back. "But he doesn't seem to be paying any attention to us. Remember, I need you to remain perfectly still."

I held my breath and tried to follow my own advice as the shark approached us. He came closer and closer, eventually passing within a couple of feet of us before executing a wide turn and submerging. The fact that I could no longer see him made me want to thrash my arms and legs, but I took my own advice and remained perfectly still.

"Where did he go?" I could hear the panic in the boy's voice.

"He's beneath us. Remember to stay perfectly still."

"What if he attacks us?"

"He won't. But if he does, you hang on to the rescue can and I'll scare him away."

"You know how to scare a shark?"

"Of course," I said with a lot more confidence than I felt. "I'm a certified lifeguard. I know everything there is about safety in the ocean."

"How are you going to scare him?" the boy asked as the shark circled just below us.

"I'm going to punch him in the nose. Sharks hate that."

The boy smiled.

It seemed like hours, but it was probably no more than a minute or two before the shark resurfaced in the distance. He swam away from us and appeared as if he was heading back to sea.

"Okay, it looks like he's gone. I'm going to swim us back to shore. We're going to go slowly so as not to make any sudden movements. I need you to remain still. Pretend you're a limp noodle."

"Okay."

"Remember, no kicking. If we see him come back we'll stop again and wait."

"Okay."

Luckily, the shark didn't come back and I was able to get us to safety without further incident. During the crisis I'd felt fairly confident, but once I was on the sand my body began to shake.

"Are you okay?" Cam asked after I'd turned Casey over to his frantic mother.

"I'm fine, although it's going to be a few minutes before my legs stop feeling wobbly. How's the victim?"

"He's on his way to the hospital. He's going to have a nasty scar, but the shark didn't do as much damage as he could have. We're going to close all the beaches in the area for the remainder of the day. Why don't you go on home?"

"Is it okay with Mitch?"

"Mitch isn't here and I haven't seen Drake for hours, so I'm making the call myself. Brody and Makena are both here and with the beaches closed, that's plenty of help."

"Okay; thanks. I wouldn't mind leaving early after my close encounter with Jaws."

"You're making a joke about it but the reality is that things could have ended very differently," Cam reminded me.

"Trust me, I've been thinking of little else."

# Chapter 9

I left the resort and went home to shower and grab Sandy. I'd called Luke earlier to warn him to stay out of the water and to let him know the gathering on the beach had been canceled. He'd invited Sandy and me to come out to the ranch for the day, and as far as I was concerned, that seemed like a perfect idea.

When we arrived I found him on the phone. He motioned for me to have a seat while he finished his conversation. "Okay, thanks. You've been a big help. I'll see you on Wednesday."

I waited for Luke to hopefully fill me in when he hung up without my having to ask him what that was all about. Not that it was any of my business, but I tended to be a snoop.

"That was Beth," Luke informed me. "It occurred to me that we might be able to figure out what Stuart was up to by following up with her lead about the house in Wahiawa."

"Follow up how? The house was completely empty."

"True, but it seemed like he might have been using the house as a cover to watch someone. I remembered it was a friend of Beth's who'd seen him coming and going, so I called her to ask if she would be willing to ask her friend about the neighbors closest to the house. She called her friend and got the names and phone numbers of the people on either side, as well as the four closest neighbors on the opposite side of the street. I thought we'd see if they'd be willing to speak to us."

"I guess it couldn't hurt, although just showing up and knocking on doors might not go over all that well."

"Which is why Beth asked her friend to call them on our behalf to set up appointments this afternoon with anyone who was available. Beth is going to call us back when she's finished. In the meantime, I made us lunch."

"You have been busy," I commented when I saw the grilled fish and fresh salads.

"It didn't take that long. Iced tea?"

"Yes, please. So if Beth is calling us back this afternoon why did you say you'd see her on Wednesday?"

"She asked me to help her hang the drapes she took down to have dry cleaned. Lemon?"

"No, thanks.

"It sounds like you had quite the exciting day," Luke said as he set the food on a tray in anticipation of taking it out onto the patio, where he'd suggested we eat.

"I guess you could put it that way, although I don't think hiding from a shark in plain sight is an event I'd like to have repeated every day. Should I grab some napkins?"

"Yeah, that would be great. It seems like you did everything just right to avoid an attack. I'm sure the boy and his parents were very grateful to you for taking a risk and heading into the water when everyone else was on the way out."

I shrugged. "That's my job. The kid was really brave. I told him to hold still and he did. It's not easy to control your emotions and remain calm when a shark is circling under you. I expected him to start freaking out at any minute."

"He trusted you and listened to what you said. I think that says a lot about your ability to do what a lot of people can't."

"I guess. Speaking of freaking out, did I tell you that Drake changed everyone's schedules all around without even discussing it with any of us?"

"Can he do that?"

"Apparently. I now have tomorrow off, but I have to work on Sunday."

"What about Monday?"

"Still off, so it won't affect our lunch and bingo plans, but now I have Saturdays, Mondays, and Wednesdays off. Not even two days in a row. I think I might quit."

"And do what?"

I had no idea. Quitting would be a rash thing to do, and even I wasn't impulsive enough to actually do it, but I was still madder than a cat in hot water and I intended to do something about the slacker as soon as I thought of something that wouldn't get me fired.

I decided to change from one painful subject to another as we settled at a table near the pool. "I noticed Courtney's car in the drive."

"She's riding with Clint."

"I thought she wanted him gone."

"She did, but then, today, she surprised me by pulling into the drive and announcing that she was going riding with him. I guess maybe he found a way to get around her anger."

"Do you think they'll get back together?"

"I doubt it, but stranger things have happened. I just hope they continue to get along. I'd prefer to stay out of their love life. I have cupcakes for dessert."

"Cupcakes! Really? That's so awesome that you remembered I love them and to go to all the trouble of serving them."

"Well, I didn't bake them or anything, but I did pick them up from the bakery. Chocolate or butterscotch?"

"Yes, please."

"Both it is."


Of the six neighbors Luke had asked Beth to have her friend talk to, three were home that afternoon, and all of them were willing to meet with us. I decided to leave Sandy with Duke and Dallas, so it was just the two of us who headed inland. Our first appointment was with a sixty-eight-year-old woman named Ellery Quinten. She'd moved to the island nine years earlier after retiring from her job as a high school principal. We'd learned that she lived alone, although she did have a son, Trevor, who lived on the mainland and visited her from time to time.

Ellery was a petite woman with a huge smile that lit up her whole face. She welcomed us with open arms, as if we were old friends come to visit and not total strangers intent on interviewing her about her familiarity with a murder victim.

Ellery's house, like its owner, was neat as a pin.

"Please have a seat." Ellery motioned to a light-colored sofa with a floral pattern that provided a perfect contrast to the solid-colored chairs across from it. "Can I get you something to drink? Iced tea? Lemonade?"

"No, thank you," I declined. "We really only want to take a moment of your time."

"Lidia said you wanted to ask about the man who'd been renting the house across the street."

Lidia must be Beth's friend. Odd that I hadn't thought to inquire about her name prior to our first interview. It really had been a long day.

"Yes. I don't know if you heard, but the man was murdered, and Luke and I are trying to help track down the killer. We visited the house but found it to be devoid of any personal possessions. We aren't sure how often he visited the house, how long he stayed, and whether or not he had visitors. We hoped the people who lived closest might provide some insight."

"I know the man you mean: the one with the suit. I'm afraid I won't be a lot of help; I do a lot of volunteer work so I'm rarely home during the day. I did see him in the evening several times, though. I thought it odd that he didn't seem to have a car. I assumed he simply walked everywhere he went, but I saw him being dropped off a block away once."

"Do you know how long he was there when you saw him arrive?"

"I'm not sure. I never saw him leave. I suppose if he was dropped off he must have been picked up as well, but I don't know for certain."

"Did you ever see him being picked up?" I asked.

"No. Just dropped off."

I remembered Stuart had met a younger man at the gas station. The attendant had told me the two had met, chatted for a bit, and then they'd left together. I assumed at the time that they'd gone somewhere together, but now it sounded like the younger guy might have just dropped Stuart off here at the house. I wondered why Stuart had left his car in the lot across from the gas station rather than just driving himself to the house. It was possible he didn't want whoever he was watching to see his car, but the house did have a garage so he could have parked inside.

"Did you ever speak to the man?"

"No. Like I said, I'm not home much during the day, and the times I saw him walk up to his porch it was late, and I wasn't about to approach a man I didn't know after dark."

"No, of course not. Can you think of anything else you might have seen that might help us understand why Stuart was spending time at the house?"

"No. I'm afraid I really don't know anything."

"And you live here alone?" Luke verified.

She nodded.

"Any recent visitors?" Luke inquired.

"My son was here for three weeks. He just left a week ago. I can give you his phone number if you want to ask him about seeing the man, but he didn't hang out at the house all that often either, so I doubt he would know anything."

"Probably not, but I wouldn't mind speaking to him anyway if you're willing to share his contact information."

We left Ellery's home with Trevor's contact information and headed next door to speak to a woman named Trixie Bell. The woman who answered the door looked to be in her midthirties, had bright red hair, a brightly colored tattoo on her neck and cheek, and black fingernails.

"Yeah?"

"Are you Trixie Bell?"

"No, Trixie is my roommate. Hang on."

She closed the door in our faces while she presumably went to fetch the woman we'd come to see.

"I wonder why Beth's friend didn't set up interviews with both women if they both live here," I said.

"I don't know. Maybe she knew the redhead wouldn't speak to us. She did seem to be a bit rough around the edges."

"I suppose. Still, I would have thought she at least would have mentioned the roommate."

I turned around and scanned the street while I waited for the door to reopen. It was a standard middle-class neighborhood, with nice if unspectacular homes that were, for the most part, well-kept-up. A lot of my friends had sought out residences in neighborhoods such as this one, but I couldn't imagine not being on the water.

"Are you Luke and Lani?" A buxom blonde with chubby cheeks and bright blue eyes asked when the door finally opened once again.

"We are," I confirmed. "And you're Trixie?"

"Yes. Come inside. I'm afraid the place is a mess, but Greta and I are out a lot so we don't always take the time to clean up."

Trixie shoved everything that had been left on an old green sofa to the floor and then kicked it out of the way prior to indicating we should take a seat. "I heard about the man across the street. Such a tragedy."

"Did you know him well?"

"No. In fact, I didn't know him at all. I did see him come and go a few times, but I never stopped to speak to him. He seemed the private sort, if you know what I mean."

"When you saw him come and go was he walking or did he have a vehicle?" I asked.

"Walking. Always walking."

"And did you ever see him speak to anyone?"

"No. He always seemed so purposeful. He'd come down the block and head directly for the house. Didn't seem the type to stop and chat. I know he did have at least one visitor, however."

"Really? Who?"

"I don't know his name and I only got a glimpse of him, he was tall, even taller than the man renting the place." Trixie paused, as if to gather her thoughts. "He had light-colored hair; not really blond but lighter than brown, and it was cut short, like one of those military cuts, and younger than the renter. I'd say he was in his midthirties. He could have been younger, I guess. Like I said, I only got a glimpse of him, but I did notice he was built. I'd say he goes to the gym frequently, or maybe he has a job that requires a lot of lifting."

"Sounds like you actually remember quite a lot," I observed.

"Yeah, maybe I do. The guy was a babe. I couldn't help but take a second look."

"And when was it you saw this man?"

"It must have been a couple of weeks ago. I work nights during the week, but I'm off on Sundays and Mondays. It would have to have been a Sunday or a Monday. It wasn't last week because I was at my cousin's wedding the entire weekend, so it must have been the week before that on Sunday or Monday."

Stuart was killed two Mondays ago, so his visitor would have to have come around on Sunday, June 19.

"How well do you know the neighbor to your right?" Luke asked.

"Ellery? Ellery and I are pretty, close considering the age difference. We're both busy, but we stop to chat whenever we run into each other. Did you know she's been to Paris, France? Not once but twice. It's always been my dream to go to Paris, France. I guess that's how we started talking in the first place. I'd moved in recently and she'd just gotten back from her second trip and I was totally interested in hearing everything about it."

"Does Ellery travel a lot?" I wondered. I don't know what that had to do with our investigation, but I found I was interested.

"She does. In fact, she'd just gotten home from Prague when her son arrived for a visit. I still haven't had a chance to get all the details."

"Tell me about the son," Luke said.

I imagine that, like me, Luke had realized the son's visit and Stuart's participation with the senior group lined up pretty darn close.

"Trevor is an odd guy. Quiet and secretive. Not at all like his mama. He has a look about him that I find uncomfortable, so I tend to avoid visiting with Ellery when he's around."

"A look?" I asked.

"You know, creepy. I heard he was in prison at one time, although I don't know that for certain. He has a lot of scars and he looks like he's lived a rough life. There's absolutely nothing soft or welcoming about the guy. Greta likes him, though; I think they hang out from time to time when he's in town, but she has that edgy thing going on, the way he does."

"Do you think she would be willing to talk to us?"

"She left just after you got here, but even if she was home I sort of doubt she'd tell you anything. She only really opens up with people in her inner circle."

"Don't take this the wrong way, but the two of you seem unlikely roommates."

Trixie laughed. "You aren't wrong; she's dark and edgy and I'm light and funny, but we share a love for all things otherworldly and supernatural. We actually met at a Comic Con in Honolulu a few years ago and have been friends ever since. If you're really interested in talking to Greta I can ask her on your behalf, but I wouldn't get my hopes up."

Luke jotted down his cell number and handed it to Trixie, then asked her to call him if Greta was open to a conversation. We spoke for a few minutes longer and then headed across the street for our last arranged interview.

The house to the right of the one Stuart had rented was occupied by a middle-aged couple with two teenage sons. The wife, Tina, was the only one at home. She was polite and friendly, although not quite as welcoming as Ellery.

"Lidia said you wanted to ask me some questions about the man who rented the house next door."

"Yes," I confirmed. "It will only take a few minutes. We're interested in the frequency with which the man stayed in the house, and how long he was there."

"I saw him come and go several times. I didn't always see him leave, but I did notice him exit through the back gate on several occasions. I guess he must have stayed for a couple of hours each time he came by."

"And did he come by very often?"

The woman shrugged. "I guess two or three times a week. He came at different times, if that helps at all. I even remember seeing him show up before sunrise one day a couple of weeks ago."

"And when he visited how did he arrive?"

"He walked. I don't think he had a car. At least I never saw one. The bus stops a few blocks from here, so I imagine he took it and then walked to the house."

"Did you ever see him in a car?"

"Actually, now that you mention it, I did. I was out late walking the dog and I saw him get into a car that was waiting at the side of the road a couple of blocks from here. I thought it odd because if someone was going to pick him up, why wouldn't they just come to the house?"

"Do you remember what kind of car it was?"

"Dark in color. A four-door sedan of some sort. I'm not good at makes and models."

"Do you remember anything at all about the car that could help us?" Luke joined into the conversation for the first time.

"The license plate. Normally I wouldn't, but it was one of those special plates for the military. My nephew served in the war in Afghanistan and he has one. Anyway, the car the man got into had one of those veterans' plates with the number T3469. My name starts with a T and my birthday is March 4, 1969, so I remembered it. I mean, what a coincidence, to have a license plate that could almost be custom made for me, except for the fact that I'm not a veteran."

This license plate number could be a huge clue. We chatted with Tina for a while longer and then I called Jason as soon as we got to the truck. I made him promise to fill me on the details as soon as he ran down the plate.

"This might wrap the whole thing up," I commented.

"Maybe. It does seem it was worth making the trip out here this afternoon."

"Should we try to speak to the other people we weren't able to make appointments with while we're here?"

Luke pulled the list out of his pocket. "We haven't talked to a young couple with two children who were both at work when Lidia called, a single man in his late twenties who lives in the house his parents left vacant after they moved to the mainland, and three women who work as flight attendants and share the space."

I wondered if the flight attendants knew Kevin and Sean. I supposed not all flight attendants from all airlines knew one another, but it could be a pretty small world and people with common jobs might at least have met.

"I guess we could knock on doors, but it might be better to wait to see what your brother turns up," Luke suggested.

"Yeah, I agree. What now?"

"Do you have plans for this evening now we aren't meeting on the party?"

"No, not a one."

"Would you like to come to the house for dinner? I'd take you out somewhere, but I have a mare that's about to foal and

I really should hang close to the house for the next twenty-four hours."

"You're having a new baby? Why didn't I know that?"

Luke shrugged. "You don't seem all that interested in the horses, so I generally avoid talking about them."

"I'm interested in baby horses. If the foal is born tonight can we watch?"

"From a distance."

Luke started the truck and headed back toward the highway. I found myself relaxing as I listened to him talk about the pregnant mare and the foal he hoped would result from carefully researched breeding. I could tell he put a lot of time and effort into choosing mated pairs based on a number of factors mainly having to do with genetic traits.

Call me ignorant, but I guess I just assumed the foals born to Luke's stable were the result of nothing more than proximity. As he explained using family histories and genetic markers to predict everything from overall health to speed and endurance, I began to see a different side to what I'd previously considered to be no more than a hobby.

"So you actually use these plans to try to correct for genetic weaknesses in a family line?"

"Yes. It doesn't always work out the way I plan, but I've been pretty successful so far. It's really a fascinating process if you're interested in learning more about it."

"Maybe. At this point I'm mostly just interested in playing with the foals. I've never seen the birth of any animal before, so I imagine that will be interesting."

"If my calculations are correct you should get to see your first animal birth before the end of the day."

"If she's due today do you think we should have left her alone to come out here?" I wondered.

"My veterinarian was by to check on her this morning. He estimated that the time of birth would be between eight p.m. tonight and eight a.m. tomorrow morning. He's never been wrong before. Besides, Charlie is around this afternoon."

"Charlie?"

"I hired him to help out with the horses a couple of months ago. He lives in the little room off the stable."

Suddenly it occurred to me that I knew very little about Luke's life outside the time we were together. He seemed to know everything about me and always asked about my work, my family, and my interests, whereas I rarely asked about his. Initially, I'd intentionally been trying to create a feeling of distance between us, but now? Now I guess I had a choice to make.

# Chapter 10

We stopped by the barn as soon as we got back to the ranch to check in on Luke's pregnant mare, which was where I met Charlie. I wondered about his last name, but he told me he liked to keep things informal, so he was just Charlie. His face was weathered, although it was impossible to tell his actual age. He walked with a swagger and talked like a cowboy, so I imagined riding the range was how he'd spent his life.

"Our little darling is doing just fine," Charlie informed Luke. "I've been sitting with her since you left. Foal seems to be in a good position, so I don't anticipate any problems."

"Thanks, Charlie. I appreciate your keeping an eye on our girl."

"I'm happy to keep an eye on her because you have a lady friend visiting. I've got nothing better to do."

I could see by the look on Luke's face that he held genuine affection for the man. "Call me the minute it looks like the foal is on the way. It's important to me to be here."

"Will do, boss. Nice to meet you, ma'am."

"He seems nice," I said to Luke as we left the barn and headed to the house.

"Charlie is a good guy. Worked for my dad for a lot of years but decided he could use a change of scenery after all this time and asked if I had work for him. Having him here has been a huge help. I wouldn't have been able to spend time with my family if Charlie and Courtney hadn't pitched in while I was away."

"Hawaii is quite a bit different from Texas. Is Charlie enjoying his time here?"

"I think he is. I doubt he'll stay forever, but he seems content for the time being."

"Does he have family anywhere?"

Luke shook his head. "He never married or had children and I've never heard him mention siblings. As far as I know, my parents, brothers, sisters, and I are the only family he has."

"And when he's ready to retire?"

"I doubt Charlie will ever actually retire, but my dad will make sure he's taken care of financially. Charlie's part of the family."

"That's nice."

Luke shrugged. "It's the way we do things. Are you hungry?"

"Actually, I am. I know it hasn't been all that long since lunch, but I guess it was a light lunch."

"I have some steaks we can grill."

"Sounds great. Can I help?"

"There's cold beer in the fridge if you want to grab us a couple."

I found the beer while Luke got the steaks and we headed out to the BBQ area located on one end of the patio. The three dogs seemed reluctant to follow us from the air-conditioned house out to the considerably warmer patio, but the sight of the steaks in Luke's hand seemed to be the deciding factor.

The outdoor kitchen was located under a terrace that blocked out the sun. There were large fans strategically placed to provide air flow even when the trade winds that normally provided a cooling affect were absent. Luke had built a small koi pond at the foot of an artful waterfall near the back of the area, which, combined with the waterfall from the pool, provided a relaxing sound.

"It's always so nice and peaceful out here," I commented as I settled into a chair in the shade.

"That was my plan when I designed the patio. I wanted something that was really more of a living space. It's nice to have an outdoor area for entertaining. My sister and her family practically lived out here when they were visiting."

"Did you have a nice visit with your sister? With all the commotion, I haven't really had a chance to ask you about it."

"It was nice," Luke said as he seasoned the steaks before setting them on the grill. "She wants me to move back to Texas and her constant hints about it got old after a while, but overall it was really good to see her. I know I moved a long way away from my family, and some might see that as an attempt to avoid them—and maybe to a certain degree it was—but I do miss them."

"Do you think you'll move back at some point?"

Luke seemed to be considering my question carefully. "I don't have any plans to or even thoughts about moving back right now. I love my life here and I'm not in any hurry to give it up, but I suppose it isn't outside the realm of possibility that I might wake up one morning and miss the wide open spaces of home."

I felt my heart sink. This was the exact reason I didn't want to become romantically involved with him. If he left my heart would break, and there was no way I would follow him the way Courtney had because I knew I could never leave my island.

"Medium rare?" Luke confirmed.

"Yes, please. You seem to always have steaks in your freezer. Do you buy them in bulk?"

"My mom sends me a case every month. I'm pretty sure she assumes there's no beef on the island." Luke chuckled. "The truth is, she sends me a lot more meat than I can eat on my own, but I think it makes her feel like she's in some way contributing to my health and well-being. Sending the meat seems to be important to her and I always have guests to help me eat what I can't."

"That's nice that your mom still wants to look out for you. I'm surprised she hasn't visited."

"She hates to fly."

"That's funny. My mom hates to fly also. My dad has been wanting to take her on a real vacation for years, but she always has an excuse why it won't work out. She doesn't even like to take the little hopper flights between islands, which is why she insists that my brothers come home and visit on a regular basis."

"How's Jeff doing with his new wife?"

My youngest brother, Jeff, had married a woman my mother wasn't at all fond of last March and things hadn't gone well when he'd brought her home for the first time after they got married. "Things are still tense. Jeff and Candy haven't visited since that first disastrous dinner and my mom claims she's fine with that, but everyone knows she isn't. Still, Jeff is insisting she apologize to Candy for the things she said and Mom flat out refuses. My dad has tried to talk to her about doing it, and my brothers have tried to get Jeff to let it go, but neither is budging. At some point one of them is going to have to give in. My brothers actually have a bet going as to which one it'll be." I looked at my phone when it beeped, letting me know I had a call. "Speaking of my brothers, it's Jason."

"I'm anxious to hear what he has to say."

"Hi, Jason, what'd you find?" I frowned as I listened to his reply. "Okay. Thanks for filling me in." I glanced at Luke. "Yeah, I will."

"So?" Luke asked.

"Jason said the man belonging to the license plate number Tina gave us was found dead in his apartment on the same Monday Stuart was killed."

"Dead?"

"A drug overdose. It seems he'd suffered from depression, so no one thought anything about it. It was considered to be an accidental overdose and there wasn't any sort of investigation. Of course, now that this man, whose name is Nick Frankford, has been associated with Stuart and he was found dead on the same day as Stuart, they're taking another look at it."

"Does it sound like this guy is the same man who was seen by the clerk at the gas station?"

"Based on the description he had, it sounds like it very well could be. Jason said the man had served in both Afghanistan and Iraq and was honorably discharged after suffering an injury to his head. When he returned home he suffered from paranoia and depression, which he seemed to be handling; still, he did self-medicate at times, so no one was overly shocked when he overdosed."

"Okay, so a man who used to be in the military had been seen with another former member of the military, and while they were a generation apart in age, they seemed to be working on something together. Why?"

"I wish I knew. The only lead we have that hasn't yet been explained is the house. What were they doing in the house? I think we need to take another look."

"It's late and I should stay with my pregnant mare."

"Tomorrow, then. Thanks to Drake's meddling, I have the entire day off. Maybe the three neighbors we didn't have the opportunity to speak to will be home tomorrow. It's Saturday."

Luke's phone beeped. He looked down at his text. "It's showtime."

Watching Luke and Charlie work side by side to help the mare deliver her foal was one of the grossest yet most beautiful things I'd ever seen. The men were so gentle and comforting, speaking to the mare the entire time as they helped the foal into the world. It wasn't an overly complicated delivery, but I still couldn't help but shed a few tears of both joy and relief when a little girl with honey-colored hair took her first breath.

"She's so cute," I gushed as I hung on to the gate of the stall and watched as mom and baby got to know each other. "What's her name?"

"I don't have one yet," Luke said. "Any suggestions?"

"Well, I'd say Lani, which means heaven, to counteract Lucifer, the first of your foals I met, but that might get confusing; I'd never know if you were talking about me or the horse. How about Hoku, which means Star? A star is a part of the heavens."

"I love it." Luke smiled. "Hoku it is."

"It's late." I yawned. "As awesome as this was, I should get home and get some sleep."

"Come by when you get up. I'll make us breakfast before we head over to Wahiawa."

# Chapter 11

## Saturday, July 2

I arrived at Luke's the next morning to find he'd made crêpes. Crêpes! How was it that a cowboy/stockbroker from Texas knew how to make crêpes? They were light and fluffy and he'd made them with a variety of different fillings. They were all delicious and I thoroughly enjoyed the meal, served, as most of the ones I'd had at the ranch, out on the patio.

"Okay, I have to ask: Where did you learn to cook like this?"

"My meemaw. She was a fabulous cook. Really gifted. She tried to teach my sisters to cook, but neither were interested, so the minute I was old enough to hold a spoon she started having me help in the kitchen. I was the youngest and our household was busy, so I found my time alone with Meemaw to be really special. Unlike my sisters, who've hired people to help out with the cooking and cleaning, I find that I really enjoy both."

"You're going to make someone a wonderful wife one day," I teased.

Luke winked at me. "That's the plan."

That wink gave me all sorts of feelings I didn't want to deal with at the moment, so I changed the subject. "How's Hoku doing today?"

"She's just fine. We can head over to visit for a spell once we're done here if you'd like."

"I would like. I know it seems odd, given the fact that I really hate horses, but I've found I really love baby horses."

"Maybe if you're around Lucifer and Hoku as they grow up you'll learn to love big horses as well," Luke suggested.

I supposed he could have a point. Lucifer had grown quite a bit in the three months since his birth and I still loved visiting with and even petting him every time I was on the property. Maybe having the opportunity to meet a horse when it was little would allow me to tolerate it a bit better once it got big.

"Do you have any other pregnant mares?" I wondered.

"Not at the moment, but I've been working on a couple of pairings I may pursue. I was hesitant to get too involved in the process until I had a chance to check out a couple of other leads I've been looking in to. Hoku was really the first paring I researched on my own, without input from my father. So far I'm happy with the results, but it's a bit early to tell how good I am at it."

"She's beautiful. I'm sure she'll be everything you hoped."

"You know, I almost didn't go with the pair I eventually chose. It's really interesting," Luke began, then continued with his train of thought for several minutes.

I could see he was really in to his goal of building a better horse. I listened and tried to understand, although some of the science Luke used to make his decision was confusing. I tried to ask the right questions and show my interest and support, but to be honest, most of it went over my head.

"I've been thinking some more about the murder investigation," Luke commented after we'd exhausted the subject of baby horses. "I think I'd like to take a look at the actual location where the murder occurred. It's been almost two weeks, so I doubt we'll find any sort of physical evidence, but it might help me get things straighter in my mind."

"We can stop by on the way to Wahiawa."

"I'll need to be back by midafternoon."

"For your big date?" I teased.

"It's not what you think."

"Actually, I'm betting it is. When I got home last night Elva poked her head out of her door and told me that you'd agreed to take her to the senior dance tonight. That was really nice of you. I know it means a lot to her."

Luke shrugged. "She needed a date. I guess initially she planned to ask Stuart; then she'd decided not to attend at all, but she got together last night with some of the gals from the center and they talked her into going. She called me, explained she didn't have a date, and asked if I would be willing to accompany her. I told her I'd be delighted."

"It's been a while since I've seen her this excited."

"Elva is a nice woman. Sort of reminds me of my meemaw."

"What time do you need to pick her up?"

"The dance is at six, but I thought I'd get her before that and take her out to an early dinner."

"It's after nine now and we want to stop at the beach and the house Stuart was renting, so we should get a move on."

Unlike the morning on which Stuart was killed, there were quite a few people on the beach and in the water. Luke found a parking space near the back of the lot and we walked over to the spot on the beach where the sunrise ceremony had been held.

"When I met Stuart he was standing right about here." I stood in the general location. "Most of the seniors were over there on the beach at the foot of the bluff. When I found out Stuart didn't have a shell to blow I left him with Elva and went to my Jeep. When I returned Elva was standing alone. She told me Stuart had walked off in that direction." I pointed to the place on the beach that led away from the bluff. "She lost sight of him once he walked around those tall shrubs and never saw him again. I later went up to the bluff to look for him and saw him floating in the water."

"But you think he was killed elsewhere?"

"I didn't at first. I thought he fell from the bluff or maybe was pushed, but I talked to everyone there that day and no one saw him go up to the bluff. It's true all eyes were on the horizon, so initially I suspected he snuck back around and accessed the bluff trail from behind the group, but Shredder explained to me that there's a strong current at this beach and it's totally possible that his body could have floated around to the spot where I found it after only a short period of time, even if he'd been killed where he was last seen."

Luke began to retrace the steps Elva had seen Stuart take, looking around the entire time. I followed him and looked around as well, although I wasn't sure what it was we were looking for. We rounded the corner where the large shrubs grew and so were no longer visible from the part of the beach where the ceremony had taken place, and Luke stopped walking.

"So whereabouts is this current Shredder referred to?"

"Based on his description, it comes around the point and flows into this little bay to about the point where those surfers are hanging out. It then flows parallel to the beach until it hits the bluff, where it flows around the landmass and back toward shore. Based on what Shredder described, Stuart would have had to have entered the current about where those surfers are now."

"That's quite a way from the beach," Luke pointed out.

"True," I had to admit.

"If Stuart was killed on the beach or just offshore his body would most likely have ended up right back here on this beach. For him to have entered the current the killer would have had to take him out there."

"True again."

"Do we know if Stuart's cause of death was drowning?" Luke asked.

"It was. I verified that with Jason."

Luke looked around. "If Stuart drowned and entered the water here, the person who drowned him would have had to have been incredibly strong. Sure, Stuart was getting on in years, but if he used to work for the military as some sort of bounty hunter, as we suspect, he would have been trained in hand-to-hand combat. It wouldn't have been easy for most men to pull him into the water, hold him under, and then swim him out to the current, let alone doing all this without being seen or heard by anyone around the bend on the beach."

"The horns are pretty loud when they're all being blown at once," I said.

"Yes, but the physical strength it would have taken to accomplish the task leads me to believe we aren't looking for another senior."

"At first I just assumed one of the seniors was guilty, but it looks like they all have alibis that check out. Elva said it seemed like Stuart was looking for someone. It did occur to me that if he was here for some sort of a meeting, arranging to meet on the beach where twenty seniors had already arranged to be didn't make a lot of sense. Especially if he wasn't here to meet a senior."

"Do you know for certain that Stuart was here for the ceremony?" Luke asked.

"No. In fact, if you take into consideration the fact that he didn't even bring a horn, it seems more likely that he hadn't planned to attend the ceremony at all. Maybe he hadn't even been aware it was being held here at this beach. It sort of makes more sense that he was here for another reason and just happened to run into Elva and me."

"Okay, then, if he wasn't here for the ceremony, who was he here to meet?"

I had no idea, but I suspected finding the answer to that question would lead us to the killer. "Let's head over to the house to see if we can come up with anything new," I said.

When we arrived at the house we found it was locked up tight, unlike the day before. We were unable to gain access without actually breaking in, so we parked on the street and tried to figure out what it was Stuart was looking for. There was a fence around the back of the house, so it seemed unlikely he'd been watching the neighbors on either side. If he was watching the homes across the street, he'd have done so by watching the window at the front of the house. The way the garage jutted out on one side probably meant only three of the homes would have been visible from that vantage point, one of which belonged to Ellery Quinten, who we'd already spoken to. I still considered Ellery's son Trevor to be a possible target; it seemed he might fit the profile of someone worth watching. The house next to Ellery's was the one being rented by the single guy in his twenties and the one next to that belonged to the three flight attendants. That last house looked to be deserted, so we decided to start with the one in the middle.

"Are you Donald Highlander?" I asked when a tall, fit man who wasn't half bad-looking answered the door.

"I am, and who might you be?" He totally ignored Luke while leering at me.

"My name is Lani and this is Luke. We wanted to ask you a few questions about the man who was renting the house across the street if you have a few minutes."

I couldn't help but notice the guarded look that flashed across his face just before he invited us inside. I suppose the fact that he was suspicious of us didn't mean he was necessarily guilty of anything. It could just be that he was cautious of anyone who was going door to door asking questions about a dead man.

The first thing I noticed when I entered the living room was a photo of him and a group of men, all in uniform, sitting on a bookshelf near a bunch of other photos. "Are you in the military?"

"Was. Served in Iraq."

"Been out long?" Luke asked.

"Is this pertinent to your investigation?"

"No," I answered because it seemed he didn't like Luke based on his defensive tone of voice. "We were just curious. Lidia mentioned this house actually belongs to your parents."

"I just got out of the service a few months ago and didn't have a place to crash, so my parents let me stay here. They moved to the mainland and aren't using the place. Now what is it you wanted?"

"We were wondering if you'd seen the man who rented the house across the street coming and going?"

"No. Not once. I didn't even know anyone was living there until the cops showed up and began asking everyone questions after the guy was whacked."

"So you didn't notice anyone at all across the street?"

"I just said that, didn't I?"

"Yes, you did. Well, thank you for your time, and thank you for your service to our country."

With that, the man showed us out and Luke and I returned to the truck.

"That wasn't much of an interview," Luke noted.

"I didn't need to ask a bunch of questions because I think I figured it out."

"Care to share what it is you figured out?"

I got into the passenger seat and Luke climbed in behind the wheel. I turned to look at him as he rolled down the windows.

"Donald said he served in Iraq. I noticed several photos set around the room of Donald in his uniform. I suppose that's normal if the place actually belongs to his parents. Anyway, in one of the photos he was standing next to a man who looked an awful lot like the man who was seen with Stuart."

"The one who overdosed?"

"One and the same. I did a search for him last night after I got home and found a photo of him. I'm pretty sure the man in the photo with Donald was him."

"Okay, so the man who seemed to be some sort of partner to Stuart knew Donald. Do you think Stuart was watching Donald?"

"I think Stuart was watching for Donald's grandfather."

Luke looked confused.

"In addition to Donald, there were photos of other people I suspect are other family members. I noticed a photo of a man who recently began going to the senior center. I've only met him a couple of times, but his name is Richard Highlander. The name didn't really click with me before, but once I saw the photo I remembered speaking with him briefly. I believe he just recently arrived on the island."

"So you think Stuart was watching the house waiting for this Richard Highlander to pay a visit to his grandson?"

"Maybe. The photo in the living room showed a much younger Richard than the one I met, dressed in an Army uniform.

What if Richard was one of the military fugitives Stuart was after? He joined the senior center and staked out the house where Donald was living in order to track the guy down."

Luke frowned. "Jason said Stuart was no longer in the military. Why would he do that?"

"Dilly mentioned something about Stuart not being here for him but being after someone else. What if Richard Highlander was someone who got away? Stuart might not be in the military any longer, but if he'd spent much time trying to track this guy down when he was, maybe he was unable or unwilling to let it go even after he went into his own business as a private investigator."

"Seems like a stretch."

"Maybe, but it also sort of fits. Donald moved to the island after he got out of the military. He moved into his parents' house and ran into Nick, an old buddy from Iraq, who came by his place and saw the photo of his grandfather. Maybe Nick knew who Richard Highlander was, so he called Stuart, who he knew through some prior association. He told Stuart a guy he'd been looking for was here on the island. Stuart came here to track Richard down, but he didn't know where he lived, so he staked out the house across the street from his grandson. At some point he must have gotten a heads-up that Richard had been seen at the senior center, so he started hanging out there as well."

"Like I said, it's a stretch. Why is it you think Stuart was after Richard and not Donald?"

"Because Donald has been sitting here the entire time. If he was the target he would have nabbed him a long time ago. The only thing that makes sense is that Richard was Stuart's target. I think I'm going to fill Jason in. Let's go by his house. He's working from home today."

The drive to the house shared by Jason, his wife Alana, and their six-year-old twins, Kale and Kala was accomplished in short order; they didn't live all that far away from where we were parked. Luckily, Jason was home when we arrived, and after I introduced Luke to Alana and the kids, I asked if we could speak to him in private. Once we were seated in his office I explained my theory.

"Seems complicated."

"Just because it's complicated doesn't mean it isn't right," I insisted.

Jason opened his desk drawer and pulled out a business card. He explained that it belonged to one of the men to whom he'd turned Dilly over. I could tell Jason wasn't totally sold on my theory, but at least he felt it held enough water to check it out further. He called the number on the card, which took him to the military police.

Whoever answered said the man he was trying to reach was off duty, so Jason was transferred to another man, who was able to confirm that Richard Highlander had been wanted for the past forty-five years for dealing in black market munitions. He also confirmed that Stuart had spent forty of those forty-five years trying to track the man down, among other things, until he'd been forced to retire after it was proven that he'd used less than humane interrogation techniques in the course of his manhunts.

"So Stuart must have been at the sunrise ceremony hoping to track down Richard Highlander, who might have been warned or might have seen him, and instead of Stuart bringing Highlander to justice, Highlander killed him," I theorized.

"It seems like a good theory," Jason agreed. "The man I spoke to assured me they'll take it from here. It looks like you beat me to the punch this time," my brother complimented me, which had me grinning from ear to ear.

"Thanks, Jason; I appreciate that." I looked at the clock. "I guess we should get going. Luke has a date."

Jason got up and shook Luke's hand. "Thank you for your help, and thanks for keeping my little sister out of trouble."

"Hey, I kept myself out of trouble," I argued.

# Chapter 12

"You look beautiful," I said to Elva, who'd gone all-out for her big date with Luke.

"I do, don't I?" Elva smiled. "I want to thank you again for letting me borrow your young man."

"He's not my young man."

Elva rolled her eyes.

"When Luke gets here I want to take a photo of the two of you before you go off on your date. We can frame it so you'll always have a memento of this night."

"We both know it's not really a date," Elva insisted.

"There are all kinds of dates. Do you know that Luke told me you remind him of his meemaw? She passed away a few years ago, but Luke talks about her as if she was one of his favorite people. She's the one who taught him to cook."

Elva smiled. "I'm honored to remind him of his meemaw. Is my hair okay?"

"It's great. Do you want to put a flower in it?"

"No, I'd just have to fuss with it all night. Do you think I should bring a purse?"

I thought about the huge purse Elva usually carried around and realized it would only serve as a burden. "Maybe we can borrow Kekoa's evening bag. It's big enough to fit a lipstick, your ID, and some money, yet it's light and small enough to tuck into the pocket of your sweater."

"Do you think I should wear a sweater? It's pretty warm."

"I'd bring one. It'll be late when you come home and you never know when a breeze is going to come up."

"You know, I think I'm starting to get nervous. I haven't been to a dance in years."

"No need to be nervous. You're going to have a blast."

"I hope so. How's my hair?"

"You already asked me that and it's fine. Just relax."

"You're right. Luke is a great guy. I have no reason to be nervous. And it's not like this is a *real* date. Just me hanging out with Luke like I have many times before."

"Exactly. It sounds like Luke is here now." Elva still looked a little nervous; excited but nervous. I hoped she'd relax and have a wonderful time.

Luke showed up at Elva's door wearing a black suit with a white dress shirt and a black tie. He was carrying a bouquet of flowers that brought tears to Elva's eyes. I couldn't help but smile as he teased Elva to get her to smile for the photos. He really was an awfully good guy.

After they left I headed to the beach to meet Cam and some of the others. It was a perfect night for surfing and I was sorry Luke was missing it, but I was happy for Elva. I was sure she was going to have the time of her life with her cowboy to see to her every need.

"It sounds like you solved the case you were working on," Shredder said.

"I believe I did."

"Do tell," Cam encouraged.

"It looks like Stuart was using the place in Wahiawa to watch the house across the street in the hope that one of the fugitives he'd been looking for would show up to visit his grandson."

"Are you talking about Donald Highlander?" Sean asked.

"Yeah. Donald is the grandson. Do you know him?"

"I don't really know him, but I've met him. We have some friends who live next door to him." I remembered the three flight attendants who shared the house next to Donald's parents'. "We were talking with one of them in the driveway as we were preparing to leave after one of our visits and Donald pulled into his own driveway. She introduced us and we chatted for a while. I mentioned I was thinking of getting my private pilot's license and Donald mentioned his grandfather used to be a pilot before his stroke."

"Stroke?"

"Yeah. He lost the use of his left side and had to give up his license."

"Are you talking about Richard Highlander?"

"Yeah, that sounds right."

"Damn. Richard was my prime suspect. I was sure he was the one who killed Stuart, but if he doesn't have the use of the left side of his body there's no way. I guess I'd better call Jason to fill him in, although I'm sure he knows this piece of information by now."

"Wow; sorry, Lani," Sean offered. "I didn't mean to burst your bubble. Want to take another run?"

I looked out at the surf. It was calling. "Yeah. Let me call Jason and I'll meet you out there."

Surprisingly, Jason hadn't heard about Richard Highlander's condition. He supposed the military were interested in him for his past crimes whether he was handicapped now or not, and because both Stuart and Nick were civilians at the time of their deaths, they probably didn't consider solving their murders to be under their jurisdiction. The fact that Richard hadn't been guilty of the murders was probably inconsequential in their detainment of him. Still, Jason felt they should have given him a courtesy call when they realized Richard wasn't the man he was looking for, unless they hadn't managed to catch up with him yet and were still unaware of his situation.

"How'd it go?" Shredder asked after I hung up.

"Okay. Turns out Jason wasn't aware of Richard Highlander's condition. He was disappointed that we probably still don't have our killer. Who's that surfing with Sean?"

"His name is Woody, or at least that's the name he goes by."

"He looks familiar."

Shredder shrugged. "He's stationed here, so you've probably seen him around."

"Stationed here? Is he military?"

"Army, I think. Why?"

"I'm not sure." And I wasn't. It just seemed like everything kept coming back to the Army, and I was sure I'd seen this man before and it hadn't been surfing. "You heading back out?"

"I could do another run or two before I head home," Shredder answered.

I looked at Cam. "How about you?"

"I have to work tomorrow. I think I'm going to call it a night."

"Same here," Kevin said. "It looks like Sean's heading in. I'm going to suggest we head home. We have an early flight in the morning."

"Okay. I'll see you guys when you get back into town."

By the time Shredder and I were going out Sean was heading in. We stopped to wish him a safe trip the following day and he told us Woody knew all about Richard Highlander. Although he was off work that day, he'd heard that the old man had been apprehended and detained. I guess it made me feel good that my meddling had resulted in not one but two arrests of military fugitives, but I still wished we'd found Stuart's killer.

Shredder and I surfed for an hour or so until the sun went down. It was a gorgeous night and the activity was helping me keep my mind off everything that was currently occupying my thoughts. I hated to come in, but it wasn't a good idea to surf after dark, especially alone, so when Shredder told me he was heading in I assured him I'd be right behind him. Shredder caught the next wave and headed toward the sand, while I sat on my board, waiting for the next perfect wave.

I was counting waves and trying to gauge when the next big wave would arrive when something—or someone—grabbed my ankle and pulled me off my board. I was so shocked I barely had time to grab a breath before I went under. I tried to kick free, but whoever had me was strong. I couldn't manage to get away, no matter how hard I tried. The harder I struggled, the more severe my need to breathe became. In the last seconds before I knew I would no longer be able to resist the urge to inhale I recognized my assailant as the man Shredder had referred to as Woody. Why was this man I didn't even know trying to kill me?

I kicked out one last time as I struggled not to breathe in water. The man was tall and well-built and he was obviously in awesome shape, but even he must be fighting the urge to breathe by now. I was close to blacking out when suddenly the man let go and I was able to swim to the surface. I was gasping for air when Shredder surfaced beside me with the man who'd attacked me secured in a head lock.

"I thought you'd left," I gasped.

"I took my board to my car, but I came back to make sure you got in okay. Sorry it took me so long."

I started to cry as I treaded water.

"Can you make it in?" Shredder asked.

"I can make it."

"Good, because there's no way I want to loosen my grip on this guy."

By the time Shredder made it to shore, Woody had passed out due to the lack of oxygen from Shredder's hold.

"Is he dead?" I asked as Sandy and Riptide licked my face, I assume to make sure I was okay.

"No. He's fine, although you'd better call 911 because I don't know what I'm going to do to this guy if he regains consciousness before HPD gets here."

"He tried to kill me. Why on earth would he try to kill me?"

Shredder shrugged. He did that a lot. At first I thought it was because he was dim, but the more I got to know him, the more certain I was that he used the shrug to avoid conversations he'd just as soon not engage in.

Woody was starting to stir by the time HPD showed up. Jason had been at home, so it took him longer to get there, but eventually he showed up as well.

"The guy in custody is from the military police. The one who picked up Dilly. The one who gave me his card," Jason said.

"The one you called earlier but was told was off today? Why would he try to kill me?"

"I have no idea, but I intend to find out. Are you okay?" Jason asked me.

"Thanks to Shredder."

Jason looked around. "Where is he?"

I looked around as well. "I guess he left after HPD showed up. He saved my life."

"We're going to want to talk to him."

"Yeah, about that...Shredder likes to keep a low profile. He risked his life to save mine. I don't want to cause him any discomfort if we don't have to."

Jason didn't argue. "Are you okay to drive?" he asked.

"Yeah, I'm fine."

"I'll follow you home before I head down to the station to have a conversation with the man who tried to kill my baby sister."

When I got home I noticed Shredder's place was dark. It made sense that he would keep to himself tonight. I had no idea what his story was, but I was certain he had one. At this point I was so grateful to him for saving my life that I didn't really care if he was a fugitive himself, which I suspected to be true although he'd denied it.

Cam and Kekoa both had to work the following morning so they'd turned in early, and it looked like Sean and Kevin's place was dark as well. I was surprised Elva wasn't home yet, but I was pretty sure she'd be home soon, so I showered and changed and Sandy and I settled onto the lanai to wait.

Ever since the attack, the reason for it had been on my mind. It occurred to me that the man who'd tried to drown me fit the description of the one Trixie had seen talking to Stuart. Every time I'd thought I had things figured out I realized I didn't. The whole thing was giving me a headache. I was about to head in and look for some aspirin when my phone rang. It was Jason.

"Hey, Jason. I didn't think you'd call. Did you get Woody to talk?"

"No. He clammed up and wouldn't say a word. The military police came to pick him up."

"Not again! Did you find out anything?"

"Actually, the MP who showed up was very cooperative and more than happy to fill me in on what he knew. It seems Stuart used to work as a sort of bounty hunter for the military. As we know, he was forced to retire when it was proven he'd used interrogation techniques that were outside of protocol to track down his fugitives. Then he went out on his own. Most of what you figured out was spot-on. He knew Nick from his days in the military, and Nick was aware Stuart regretted he was never able to track down Richard Highlander. When Nick realized Richard was here on the island he contacted Stuart who made the trip over at his first opportunity. It took Stuart a while to track down Richard, but when he did, he decided to do the right thing and turn him over to the military, so he called and spoke to Woody."

I remembered the phone number on the gum wrapper.

"Woody met Stuart at the house and Stuart told him everything he knew. Woody promised to let him be in on the take-down, which was why Stuart was on the beach the morning of the ceremony. He thought he was there to take down Richard, but Woody killed him and then Nick."

"But why?"

"It seems Woody is even dirtier than the men and women he was hired to track down. It happens. He knew Richard was connected, and that he knew stuff about him that wouldn't go over well if anyone found out. He couldn't afford for Richard to be brought in and interrogated, so he warned Richard to get out of town and killed the two men intent on finding him."

Wow. Talk about twisted. "But why did he try to kill me?"

"I don't know. The man I spoke to didn't know. You said you saw him speaking to Sean about Richard; chances are he was led to believe you knew more about what was going on than you actually did. You were the last one on the water, the beach was deserted, the guy probably figured it was a low-risk way to get you out of the way just in case you did know more than he was comfortable with. This whole thing would have gone down a lot differently if Shredder hadn't come back to check on you."

"Tell me about it."

"At this point I don't think he has anything to add to our investigation so I won't bother him, but I want you to be careful. The man saved your life and for that I owe him, but he has a secret, and in the end we may end up on different sides of that secret."

"Yeah, I know. I'll be careful. Luke just pulled up with Elva. I should go. I'll talk to you tomorrow."

"Okay, little sis. *Mau moe'uhane nahenahe.*"

"Sweet dreams to you as well, big brother."

I hung up and I watched from a distance as Luke walked Elva to her door, kissed her cheek, and wished her good night. I wasn't sure he'd seen me because I was sitting on the far end of the lanai, closest to the beach, but he walked in my direction after Elva went inside.

"You're home awful late. I'm pretty sure it's past Elva's curfew," I teased.

"I took her and a few of the others out for dessert after the dance."

"That was nice of you. I'm sure they all appreciated it."

Luke slipped off his jacket and unknotted his tie. "We had a nice evening. Who knew the seniors were such partiers?"

"Did the old ladies dance you into the dance floor?"

"They did at that, but I had a wonderful time. I'm really glad Elva asked me. You know, I've lived here for two years and

I'm pretty sure this was my first real date since I came here."

I laughed. "Really? Your first?"

"Unless you want to count our meals out, which I don't. Having said that, I would very much like to take you out. On a real date. I'll pick you up, take you somewhere nice, bring you home, and, if you'll let me, kiss you at your door."

"You're asking me out?" It seemed obvious he was, but that was the only thing I could think of to say.

"I am. How about tomorrow?"

"I work tomorrow."

"Okay then, how about tomorrow after you get off work? We can go anywhere you like."

I wanted to say no. I really should have said no. There was a part of me that felt this was the perfect time for me to explain to Luke how I felt about broken hearts when the haole in your life eventually returned home. But somehow, sitting in the still night with the sound of the waves crashing onto the beach for a backdrop, I found I really wanted to go out with Luke on a real date.

"Okay," I said after a bit.

"Okay? Really?"

"I'll go out with you tomorrow on a real date on one condition."

"Which is?"

I turned and looked him directly in the eye. I leaned in close so that my lips were inches from his. "How about we start with that kiss rather than leaving it to the end?"

Luke closed the distance between us and I was pretty sure my life would never be the same.

# Recipes

## Recipes from Kathi Daley

Potato Mac Salad
Rice Salad
Easy Pineapple Upside-Down Cake

## Recipes from Readers

Island Mango Orange Cole Slaw—submitted by Jeannie
Daniel
Cabbage Casserole—submitted by Janel Flynn
Banana Pudding—submitted by Wanda Philmon Downs
Apple Kuchen—submitted by Pam Curran

# Potato Mac Salad

Potato Mac Salad is a popular side dish in Hawaii. In fact, it's one of my husband's favorites.


6 large potatoes, boiled, skinned, and diced
1½ cups elbow macaroni, cooked and drained
6 large eggs, boiled hard, peeled, and diced
1½ cups mayonnaise
Hot dog relish with mustard, ½ cup or more to taste
Lawry's Seasoned Salt, Pepper, and Paprika to taste

Combine all ingredients and refrigerate.

Note: True Hawaiian Potato Mac doesn't have the relish, but my family likes it; try it either way.

# Rice Salad

2 cups chicken broth
1 cup long grain rice
¾ cup pineapple chunks
¾ cup mango chunks
1 apple, chopped
½ cup chopped macadamia nuts

Bring chicken broth to boil.
Cook rice until done.
Add fruit and nuts.
Add dressing for additional flavor.
Mix in a commercial pineapple dressing or combine honey and pineapple juice to make a sweet dressing until desired level of moistness.

# Easy Pineapple Upside-Down Cake

¼ cup butter or margarine
1 cup brown sugar, packed
1 can (20 oz.) pineapple slices in juice, drained, juice reserved
1 jar (6 oz.) maraschino cherries without stems, drained
1 box yellow cake mix, eggs, and oil called for on box

Heat oven to 350 degrees. In 9 x 13-inch pan, melt butter in oven. Sprinkle brown sugar evenly over butter. Arrange pineapple slices on brown sugar. Place cherry in center of each pineapple slice and arrange remaining cherries around slices; press gently into brown sugar.

Add enough water to reserved pineapple juice to match liquid called for on cake mix box. Make batter as directed on box, substituting pineapple juice mixture for the water. Pour batter over pineapple and cherries.

Bake 42 to 48 minutes (44 to 53 minutes for dark or nonstick pan) or until toothpick inserted in center comes out clean. Immediately run knife around side of pan to loosen cake. Place heatproof serving plate upside down onto pan; turn plate and pan over. Leave pan over cake 5 minutes so brown sugar topping can drizzle over cake; remove pan. Cool 30 minutes. Serve warm or cool. Store covered in refrigerator.

# Island Mango Mandarin Orange Cole Slaw

## Submitted by Jeannie Daniel

1 head cabbage, finely shredded
1 carrot, peeled and finely shredded
½ cup mayo (add more or less depending on how creamy you like it)
⅓ cup sugar
3 tbs. white vinegar
Salt and pepper to taste
1 small can mandarin orange slices (drained)
1 ripe mango, cubed

Mix all the ingredients except the oranges and mango well. After mixture is mixed well, fold in the oranges and the mango. Refrigerate until ready to serve.

# Cabbage Casserole

## Submitted by Janel Flynn

The following recipe is one my great-aunt Mary Etta makes all the time.

1 large head cabbage (about 12 cups)
1 onion, chopped
6 tbs. butter
1 can cream of mushroom soup, undiluted
8 oz. American cheese, cubed
Salt and pepper to taste
⅓ cup dry bread crumbs
☐
Cook cabbage in salted water until tender; drain thoroughly. Sauté onion in 5 tbs. butter until tender. Add soup and mix well; add cheese and stir until cheese is melted. Remove from heat, stir in cabbage, salt, and pepper. Put in 2-qt. baking dish. Melt butter and crumbs together and sprinkle over casserole.☐Bake uncovered at 350 degrees for 20–30 minutes.

Makes 6 to 8 servings

# Banana Pudding

## Submitted by Wanda Philmon Downs

1 large box vanilla pudding
1 box vanilla wafers
Bananas (at least two)

Mix pudding according to instructions.

Lay wafers across bottom of dish, saving some for the top.

Slice bananas and lay over wafers.

Pour part of pudding over wafers.

Repeat with more wafers and bananas and pudding.

Place some crushed or whole wafers on top.

# Apple Kuchen

## Submitted by Pam Curran

This one came from one of many teachers I taught with years ago.  A quick dessert for teachers.

1 yellow cake mix
½ cup coconut
1 stick margarine or butter

Mix the above until crumbly.

Pat into a 9 x13-inch pan.  Bake for 10 minutes at 350 degrees.

Place 1 drained can of sliced apples on top.

Mix ½ cup sugar and 2 tsp. cinnamon together. Sprinkle over apples.

Beat 1 egg into 8-oz, carton of sour cream. Drizzle on top.

Bake for 25 minutes in a 350-degree oven. Yum!!

# Books by Kathi Daley

Come for the murder, stay
for the romance.

## Zoe Donovan Cozy Mystery:

Halloween Hijinks
The Trouble With Turkeys
Christmas Crazy
Cupid's Curse
Big Bunny Bump-off
Beach Blanket Barbie
Maui Madness
Derby Divas
Haunted Hamlet
Turkeys, Tuxes, and Tabbies
Christmas Cozy
Alaskan Alliance
Matrimony Meltdown
Soul Surrender
Heavenly Honeymoon
Hopscotch Homicide
Ghostly Graveyard
Santa Sleuth
Shamrock Shenanigans
Kitten Kaboodle

# Tj Jensen Paradise Lake Series

Pumpkins in Paradise – Sept. 2016
Snowmen in Paradise – Sept 2016
Bikinis in Paradise – Sept 2016
Christmas in Paradise – Sept 2016
Puppies in Paradise – Sept 2016
Halloween in Paradise – Sept 2016
Treasure in Paradise – April 2017

# Whales and Tails Cozy Mystery:

Romeow and Juliet
The Mad Catter
Grimm's Furry Tail
Much Ado About Felines
Legend of Tabby Hollow
Cat of Christmas Past
A Tale of Two Tabbies
The Great Catsby – *July 2016*

# Seacliff High Mystery:

The Secret
The Curse
The Relic
The Conspiracy
The Grudge

# Sand and Sea Hawaiian Mystery:

Murder at Dolphin Bay
Murder at Sunrise

# Road to Christmas Romance:

Road to Christmas Past

Kathi Daley lives with her husband, kids, grandkids, and Bernese mountain dogs in beautiful Lake Tahoe. When she isn't writing, she likes to read (preferably at the beach or by the fire), cook (preferably something with chocolate or cheese), and garden (planting and planning, not weeding). She also enjoys spending time on the water when she's not hiking, biking, or snowshoeing the miles of desolate trails surrounding her home.

Kathi uses the mountain setting in which she lives, along with the animals (wild and domestic) that share her home, as inspiration for her cozy mysteries.

She currently writes five series: Zoe Donovan Cozy Mysteries, Whales and Tails Island Mysteries, Sand and Sea Hawaiian Mysteries, Tj Jensen Paradise Lake Mysteries and Seacliff High Teen Mysteries.